HUMBLING HER COWBOY

MILLER BROTHERS OF TEXAS BOOK ONE

NATALIE DEAN

DEDICATION

I'd like to dedicate this book to YOU! The readers of my books. Without your interest in reading these heartwarming stories of love, I wouldn't have made it this far. So thank you so much for taking the time to read any and hopefully all of my books.

And I can't leave out my wonderful mother, son, sister, and Auntie. I love you all, and thank you for helping me make this happen.

Most of all, I thank God for blessing me on this endeavor.

OTHER BOOKS BY NATALIE DEAN

CONTEMPORARY ROMANCE

Miller Family Saga

BROTHERS OF MILLER RANCH

Miller Family Saga Series 1

Her Second Chance Cowboy

Saving Her Cowboy

Her Rival Cowboy

Her Fake-Fiance Cowboy Protector

Taming Her Cowboy Billionaire

Brothers of Miller Ranch Complete Collection

MILLER BROTHERS OF TEXAS

Miller Family Saga Series 2

The New Cowboy at Miller Ranch Prologue

Humbling Her Cowboy

In Debt to the Cowboy

The Cowboy Falls for the Veterinarian

Almost Fired by the Cowboy

Faking a Date with Her Cowboy Boss

Miller Brothers of Texas Complete Collection

BRIDES OF MILLER RANCH, N.M.

Miller Family Saga Series 3

Cowgirl Fallin' for the Single Dad

Cowgirl Fallin' for the Ranch Hand

Cowgirl Fallin' for the Neighbor

Cowgirl Fallin' for the Miller Brother

Cowgirl Fallin' for Her Best Friend's Brother

Cowboy Fallin' in Love Again

Brides of Miller Ranch Complete Collection

Miller Family Wrap-up Story

(An update on all your favorite characters!)

~

Copper Creek Romances

BAKER BROTHERS OF COPPER CREEK

Copper Creek Romances Series I

Cowboys & Protective Ways

Cowboys & Crushes

Cowboys & Christmas Kisses

Cowboys & Broken Hearts

Cowboys & Second Chances

Cowboys & Wedding Woes

Cowboys' Mom Finds Love

Baker Brothers of Copper Creek Complete Collection

CALLAHANS OF COPPER CREEK

Though I try to keep this list updated in each book, you may also visit my website nataliedeanauthor.com for the most up to date information on my book list.

CONTENTS

1
____

Solomon

"And remember to keep your eye out for that Annie Haynes. She's a real viper. She'll be on the lookout for anything to say we're out-of-touch billionaires trying to buy our way into heaven."

"Yes, Dad," Solomon said for what felt like the fifteenth time on the call. Unfortunately, the drive to the city from their estate was a good hour long, so Dad had plenty of time to micromanage his second eldest son.

Solomon almost wanted to tell his father to go to the grand opening of the reconstructed megachurch himself. After all, they had helped fund the rebuilding after a terrible storm damaged it the previous year. And Dad was still the patriarch in charge. But Solomon knew it wasn't worth the hassle. As the eldest son who worked on the ranch, he was due to inherit the company when Dad eventually did pass, so he needed to learn how to handle these things. And get his father to trust that he could manage the business.

Solomon normally didn't mind that. He liked the challenge of his father's world. All the negotiating and envisioning the future. Investing and mergers. Risk and reward. But what he hated was doing things just for the sake of his father's ego, and his investment in the megachurch had been just that.

Because before the disaster, it had been one of Dad's old-time rivals that had been the patron of the church, reaping in all the goodwill and tax write-offs like a champ. Solomon was under no illusion that that was exactly why his father had gotten involved. And—while he didn't really care—he wasn't exactly thrilled that *he* was the one who had to go and speak at the dinner to celebrate its refurbishment.

It was times like this that he missed his younger years, when things had been simpler and more about the ranch. Sure, while they had never been as backwater or as manual as his cousins up in the Midwest, there used to be a lot more to do with the animals and the day-to-day function. Nowadays, Solomon felt like he was in a suit more often than he was on a horse.

He would have to remedy that soon. Maybe once spring hit and things started to bloom again. He knew Mom wanted to expand her greenhouse's capabilities on the ranch. Maybe he could drive her the short distance from their estate and see what kind of hard work he could get into.

He let out a bit of a snort at that. His father would probably have a cow at the thought that his second-oldest son and heir to his empire was debasing himself with manual labor. Especially since he was so testy about Samuel deciding to stay with their Miller cousins up north. Not that Solomon blamed the eldest brother. Sammy had pretty much been criticized since he was old enough to shake a stick, never being quite what Dad wanted, and Solomon was glad that he had gotten away from it.

However, he wasn't so hot on the fact that he and all of his remaining brothers were experiencing Dad's surliness over what he considered an outright betrayal.

Ugh, that man and his ego. If it wasn't for his billion-dollar empire, Solomon was pretty sure that Dad wouldn't have any friends or followers. As it were, he doubted that McLintoc Miller had any real friends. Only yes-men and sycophants.

When Solomon eventually took over the family business, he liked to think that he would change a few things. Maybe withdraw from the social aspect and the politics of being one of Texas' most elite industrial ranches and just focus purely on the business aspect. After all, there were some lands that he had been eyeing that could be pretty heavy with resources, and he was interested in expanding into the energy trade.

...but all of that would have to wait for Dad to croak first. Not that Solomon minded his father being here. He wasn't looking *forward* to the strict man's death, but he wouldn't exactly be devastated when it happened either.

Mom was the heart of the McLintoc Miller empire, really, and Solomon knew she would support any changes he made.

"Remember, you cannot screw this up. This is your first big appearance with these people. You've done great on the business front, and I know you've set up quite the network for us, but this is different. These people hold power, real power. Something that might come in handy around election time."

Solomon withheld a sigh. There was his father talking about the elections again. He was dead set on getting some friend of his into a local seat, and Solomon couldn't care less.

Dad called him a friend but didn't really have friends. He had business partners and interests, and that was about it.

"We already discussed this before I left. And yesterday. I assure you, I will behave myself."

"You always do, Solomon. That's why I chose you, you know. You're not the eldest, but I know you're the one I can count on to lead us in the right direction."

Solomon made an affirmative noise, never really sure of how to respond to a compliment from his father. Mostly because agreeing felt like bragging, and he hated bragging. It was a point of contention he often had with his second-youngest brother, who built his whole persona on top of being one of the filthy rich Millers of Texas.

Granted, Solomon didn't feel like he had anything outside of the family, but that was just because so much work went into being the next generation leader of their father's empire. There were business mergers and investments, and the automation of the massive ranch Dad had built from the ground up.

Of course he never would have been able to even get started if it weren't for the wealth from Grandpappy, a man Solomon had only met once. The Millers had been rich for generations, really, wealth building on wealth. But sometime in his twenties, Dad had decided that he was tired of all the waste and lack of profit that went into running a family-owned ranch with almost zero automation. He had set off on his own.

Solomon got why. Dad didn't like being second fiddle to anyone, and when he realized he wasn't going to become the head of the business, it probably grated him in all the wrong ways. Solomon also didn't think it was a coincidence that Dad's business was basically the polar opposite of Grandpappy and Uncle Douglas' ranches.

Uncle Douglas Miller and Dad still had a lot of contention about that particular matter. Dad thought Uncle Douglas was an idiot of a hippie, and Uncle Douglas made it clear he was concerned about how Dad treated his animals. It was an age-old debate that, honestly, Solomon was tired of.

Lately he felt so tired of everything.

"I'm going to concentrate on my drive the rest of the way. You know how traffic gets going into the city."

"Yeah, right. Keep your eyes on the road. Do us proud."

The line clicked off and Solomon sagged in his seat. Ugh, hopefully the church would be less taxing than more business conversations with his own father.

... it wasn't.

From almost the first moment he was out of his truck, people were fawning all over him. He vaguely recognized them, offering calm and professional greetings while they shook his hand and generally invaded his personal space. They said thank you and rattled off what was great about their megachurch, and Solomon couldn't help but find it all so shallow.

Strange, he'd been a Christian for as long as he could remember, going to Sunday School way before he even knew how to read the Bible that they were teaching. When he was younger it had been comforting. Giving him some reasons for things that didn't make sense. And spending time with his brothers, Mom, and friends at the local church had been fun, heartwarming even. It had given him a sense of belonging. But nowadays... nowadays it just felt so transactional to him. His family rebuilt their church after a bad storm had damaged things; the church would then throw their support behind any politics that his family supported. It was all A plus B equals C.

But maybe that was just him. As he took on more responsibilities with the ranch, he had less and less time and emotions for everything else. He couldn't even remember the last time that he had ridden his horse or done any sort of physical labor around the premises.

Somehow, he managed to keep his expression both pleasant and enthused over the entire tour—and it was a *lengthy* one. The church was oversized, ostentatious, and beautiful, all things that his father loved. Solomon had no doubt that they would be visiting the church around one Sunday a month on one of the rare weeks their father managed to wrangle them all together.

Or for any important press events.

Too bad he wasn't going to get a break anytime soon. Because after the tour, came the celebratory dinner.

And of course, it wouldn't be a dinner without a speaker, and he was the one who was supposed to give the speech. One about community, when he and his family lived at least an hour away from the city limits. About humility, when the church around him made literally millions of dollars that went into furnishing it and decorating it.

But he did just that, because that was business. He was representing the best that they hoped the church could be, not dwelling on the emptiness of it all. Not commenting on how it was all so businesslike that Jesus might have come in and flipped tables.

Because that wasn't Solomon's role. He was his father's son, after all, and his job was to make sure the business thrived. To honor his father and all the blood, sweat, and tears that had gone into building a billion-dollar ranch. *That* was his purpose.

So, he was going to be darn good at it.

2

Solomon

*I*t was a relief to finally leave the church, and he practically peeled out to get back onto the road. Perhaps he broke a few speed limits, but he was sure that he could pay whatever ticket he got *if* he got one. It wasn't like there was a plethora of cops out on the long, lone stretch of highway leading to their estate.

But he was just under halfway there when his truck dash rang, notifying him that someone was calling. He was all set to ignore it, but then he recognized the name on the display as his contact at the megachurch.

"Hello?" he asked, dreading what they could possibly want on the other end.

"Hey, we hate to be a bother, but while we were cleaning, we found something we think is yours. It's a lovely watch with your family name engraved on it."

Holy crap, his heirloom watch! He usually only wore it for dressy occasions, but it was incredibly valuable to him. A quick glance to his wrist confirmed that it wasn't there, and he chided himself for being careless.

"We think the clasp broke, judging by the looks of it. If you're willing to wait until tomorrow, we can drive it out to you. But if you want to get it tonight, we'll stay as long as you need."

He knew that the parishioners would most likely get it to him safe and sound the next day, but he didn't want to be that long without it. He couldn't believe that he hadn't noticed its absence in the first place.

Stepping on the gas, he floored it, going even faster headed back to the church than he had when leaving. He actually made it back in good time, but he was so busy slowing down to the proper city speed limit that he didn't notice his GPS telling him to turn until it was too late.

Oh well, not the hugest deal. He quickly turned onto the next street, going around in a wide circle so that he came up into the back parking lot of the church instead of the front.

It wouldn't be a big deal, he was sure. He would just call them and tell them that he was in the back, so they could bring his watch back there. Five minutes, maybe, then he would be back on the road again and *really* on his way home.

He was just getting out of his truck when he noticed a dark shape standing on top of a garbage can that had been hauled next to one of the massive walls. The person's movements were liquid, strange, but they still struck him as nothing that could be good.

He took another step closer, leaving his truck door open, and his mind deciphered more things. The form was spray painting something on the wall. Something that looked a lot like a thin, ragged child who was standing in front of a fat priest absolutely encrusted in jewels and gold. He held a gilded platter that was overflowing with food, all of it looking delectable despite the fact that it had obviously been hastily spray-painted in the forty minutes or so that he had been gone.

He wasn't going to just stand there and watch someone spray-paint graffiti all over the church walls.

"Hey! You!" he called, putting all the authority he could into his voice.

The figure reacted instantly, falling to the ground and kicking over the garbage can in their haste. It would have been satisfying to watch if the hooligan didn't immediately roll forward as soon as their body touched the dirt and spring onto their feet to run away.

"Stop! You need to clean this up!"

Before Solomon even thought about it, he took off after the figure, his adrenaline kicking into high gear at the thought of a chase. They were clearly in the lead, but he was most certainly faster, and he quickly began to close in on their baggy form.

Or at least he was until they suddenly jumped to the side, rolling over the hedges that lined the church property and streaking right across the street.

"Hey!" he called again, but the figure didn't falter.

He knew he didn't need to give chase. That he should either call the cops or let him go—after all, all it would take was a nice pressure washer to erase whatever they painted—but something in him wouldn't let his feet slow to a stop.

When was the last time he had gotten to do something so physical? When had he had such a challenge that made his lungs burn and his blood surge inside of him? He felt alive, in a really bizarre way, and perhaps he should examine why.

...another time. He was busy.

Once more he was gaining on the figure, but they darted

down an alley, turning on their heel almost like a dancer. He managed to skid and turn as well, although his arm and shoulder crashed into the wall of one of the buildings.

Whoever it was, it was clear he knew where he was going. He darted, ducked, and used shortcuts that Solomon had no idea existed. He was a city denizen, that was for sure, and he was clearly headed somewhere specific.

But still he ran, and finally they hit a straightaway, the figure booking it toward something or somewhere, but Solomon couldn't make anything out in the dark beyond the streetlights. It was his chance to cut the final bit of distance between them.

So, he took a deep breath and put his everything into running. He called back on his time in high school, when he'd been into just about every sport imaginable, controlling his breathing and form as adrenaline pumped through him.

Closer. Closer. *Closer.*

Then finally! Yes! He reached out, his hand gripping the back of the loose, black hoody and ripping it backward.

There were several things that he expected to happen. One, for the runner to jerk to a stop, secondly, to be able to stop running himself.

But neither of those things happened. Instead, the vandal twisted and jerked, never losing momentum and moving in such a way that their oversized hoody just swept off over their head. The sudden lack of weight had Solomon nearly toppling forward, and he almost crashed right into the dirt.

Stumbling, he caught himself, and a few footfalls later he managed to get his legs under him and stand, still holding onto the piece of clothing.

Solomon stared at it incredulously, trying to figure out why there wasn't a person inside of it, but the distinct sound of someone climbing a fence caught his attention.

He looked forward just in time to see the runner land on the ground in a crouch, a *very* tall chain-link fence between them. The runner rose to their feet, seemingly just as surprised as he was by the situation, and finally turned to face him.

If Solomon wasn't already shocked and confused, he definitely would have been then. Because it wasn't some gang-banger staring at him. Or hardened criminal. Or even young delinquent. No, instead it was a young woman in front of him, her dark, dark eyes wide, her cheeks flushed red while the rest of her face was a light amber and her chest heaving in the tank top she wore. Her hair was wild, electric blue and green, very noticeable in the dark of the night, and her clothes had the deliberate grunge that seemed so popular lately.

She was pretty—no, *stunning*—but it was the expression in her face that jolted him. She looked terrified, all caught up in the chase as well, but there was an edge of triumph to it. Like he had just challenged her and lost.

Which he supposed he had.

"Who the hell are you?" he heard himself asking, completely incredulous at everything that had happened.

The triumphant look in her eye only grew that much stronger and her pink, full lips curled into a smirk. For a moment, he thought that she was going to answer him, but instead she just flipped him off, her fingernail chipped but painted a nuclear green.

He opened his mouth to demand something more, politeness, or an apology, he didn't really know, but she just laughed and darted off, quickly disappearing into the large, abandoned building behind the fence.

No, *no!* Solomon roared back to life, his body taking off on its own. He ran to the nearest gate but found that it was chained and padlocked, far too much for him to do anything about.

Cursing, he stood there for several moments, his own breath harsh in his throat, before his hands finally dropped to his sides.

Whoever that woman was, she was gone, and he wasn't going to find her. He needed to go get his watch and tell the church about the graffiti, so maybe they could scrub it off before it truly set in. But as he made his way to all those shallow people and their shallow building, her image burned itself into his head.

Was she even real?

She certainly didn't seem like it.

3

———

Frenchie

𝓕renchie was cold.

Not even the pleasant cold that came after sledding and laughing with friends, followed by hot cocoa and huddling by a nice fire. No, it was the joint-achy, biting cold that sank into her bones and didn't want to leave, making everything wet and miserable.

It was September, so she didn't know what she expected. The nights were getting breezy, but she would have been fine if she hadn't lost her only protection to that strange jerk who had tailed her the night before.

She couldn't believe that happened. She'd just been tagging one of the most hypocritical churches in the whole city, not committing murder or arson. After all, they ran a food pantry and several charities *supposedly*, but all of her friends that went there were always turned away or chased off the premises.

So much for being kind to the poor or showing Jesus' love. As far as she could tell, the big fancy church and almost all of its attendants worshipped money more than that God they always talked about. Which was a shame; he seemed like a nice guy. Or at least his son was. She wasn't quite sure on a lot of the details.

She shivered again and sighed, rising from where she had been crouched down to eat her last granola bar. The best way to stay warm was to keep moving, so she might as well get going.

She didn't have a set plan for the day, but getting some food inside of herself would definitely be helpful. Rubbing her arms, she headed towards a nearby bakery, one that she knew gave away stale bagels at their close.

And thankfully, she was friendly with the owner and knew that he always set some aside for her. There was a pretty high demand for his scraps considering the quality of his food, so she was pleased as punch that all it had taken was some general politeness and a sketch she drew of his sweet, older wife once to get on his goody list.

She just wished she had her hoody.

By the time she got to the bakery, she was chilled, her fingertips aching. She didn't know what she'd do by winter if she didn't get something warmer. Hopefully there would be a coat charity drive, and then she could get a secondhand jacket.

"Hey there, Mr. Vanicotti. Ya got anything for me?"

The elderly man looked over the counter, his grandson busy wiping everything down for close. "Ah, my Francesca! It is always so good to see you! You haven't been visiting much lately, no?"

"I had a gig traveling for a couple of weeks," she said with a smile. "Was fed the entire time."

"Oh really? Not enough. You need more. Too skinny."

She laughed, wondering if she let him get away with saying that because he was old or his accent made him so lovable. "You think everyone is too skinny, Mr. Vanicotti."

"Not my wife! She is perfect in every way. You should be like her. Have man treat you right, get fat."

Frenchie laughed again. "I'd love to get fat, but you know how it is nowadays. Protein is expensive and you can only eat so many carbs."

He huffed. "I have never heard such blasphemy. This is why you're too thin. Everyone needs more pasta."

"All right, all right, I get it. I'll do my best."

Frenchie normally would never stand for someone shaming her body, but in truth she was thinner than she liked to be. She could see it in her face in the reflections on windows and in the mirrors of gas station bathrooms. Her skin hung a little too much on her, and her once-full muscles were withering.

She'd always had an athletic figure, loving sports and dance, but she could feel herself wasting away. If she didn't get a better diet soon, she was pretty sure she would become unrecognizable.

Which would be a shame. She liked herself most of the time.

"Well here, these will help. I made sure to save all your favorites that don't sell." He went to hand the bag to her, then paused. "Wait here one moment. I return."

For the slightest of moments, she was worried that he was going to leave her high and dry as he shuffled to the back, but it was only a few minutes later that he was returning, the bag looking slightly fuller.

"You take this and be careful now. Is getting cold. Where is coat?"

"I must have left it at home," she said with a bit of a chuckle.

"Ah, don't do that. You must take care of you. Too skinny, no heat."

"No heat is right." She held up the bag. "Thanks for everything, Mr. Vanicotti."

"Of course, sometime come for dinner, yes? My wife yells at me every time you go."

She chuckled at that, but then apprehension crawled up her spine. It was one thing to accept food from a kind stranger; it was another entirely to go into their home and be stuck there in unknown territory. "Maybe in a bit. I've got some errands to do."

"Right, right. You always so busy. I think you maybe run the city."

"Hah, maybe I do."

"If that's so, what am I doing giving you free bagels? It's you who should be giving me free things, yes?"

They shared a laugh, the mounting tension broken, and Frenchie excused herself before it could go uncomfortable again.

In part of her mind, she knew she likely had nothing to worry about from the Vanicottis. But another part of her mind reminded her of just how many times she had trusted people before and how it had ended up hurting her. There was only so much a girl could fall for before things started to become her fault, and she wasn't interested in continuing to be life's fool.

She pulled one of the bagels out of the bag before shoving

the rest into her backpack. It wouldn't necessarily end well for her if someone saw she had so much food all at once. They could take it, or maybe think she had actual money on her to buy things. Neither of those situations would work out for her, so she preferred to eliminate them entirely. Perhaps some would call her overcautious, but she found there was rarely such a thing as overcautious when one was a young, unaccompanied woman in the city. Especially a woman with a knack for trouble.

Frenchie smiled crookedly to herself as she made her way to the park. It wasn't that she went *looking* to make mischief intentionally. Often, she was too exhausted for anything of the sort. But there were certain times when all the drudgery, all the constant chasing down money was too much for her and she needed to do *something* to strike out at all the hypocrisy and inequality in the world.

But she wasn't smart, she wasn't well-spoken, so her tagging would have to do. Besides, it wasn't like that ridiculously rich church wouldn't be able to fix it the very next day. It was unlikely they would even understand her message. A lot of those rich types were so detached from reality that they didn't understand what it was like for the majority of the population.

She reached the park, her skin prickling from the cold. But enjoying the mildly stale bagel was mostly overpowering the unpleasant sensation. Casually, she ambled to one of her favorite spots, a wooden bench overlooking one of the many popular walking paths of the park. There was a weeping willow behind it that dramatically cut the windchill during the cooler months and provided shade during the hottest parts of the year. There were almost always people walking along the path or sitting on benches along it, so she always had subjects to draw.

She scanned the area, looking for something to inspire her. It didn't take her long to find a pregnant young woman who looked like she was in her early twenties. She had her hair up in a messy bun and was sitting contentedly, her eyes closed and her hands on her stomach. She looked so peaceful, so full of energy and something magical, that Frenchie immediately put her pencil to her paper, pausing only to put her headphones on and start her music.

Perhaps there were better things for her to do than draw. Maybe she should have been busking, or even begging for some change, but sometimes drawing felt like the only proof that she actually existed. That she mattered in the world and had any sort of effect on reality. Far too often it was so easy to feel like she was detached from society. Just some sort of castoff that life had decided wasn't worth it but wasn't kind enough to get rid of.

She continued to muse as she drew, her pencil flying across the page. She wondered if she was always meant to be an observer, always on the outside of everything. Or if somewhere in the grand, cold world, there was something more meant for her.

But she should know better than that. Daydreaming about something more always left her feeling worse than before. Hope was a dangerous drug in her profession.

4

———

Solomon

Solomon couldn't get the girl out of his head.

Which was crazy. And he knew it was crazy. And yet, that was exactly what was happening.

He told himself that he was mad that she was defacing property that his family had put so much money into. That her vandalism was a direct mark on his father and their legacy. That she was some hooligan trying to entertain herself by ruining something others worked on.

But none of those things rang true.

Not that he knew *why* the girl wouldn't get out of his head. He just knew that she was stubbornly embedded in his thoughts.

His phone buzzed, and he checked it to see it was a picture message from Samuel. Opening it, he saw a happy selfie of his eldest brother and his new girlfriend, a poor farm hand from

Aunt Annie's and Uncle Douglas' Miller Ranch up in Montana. Dad was absolutely livid about it, but Solomon thought it made sense.

He saved the picture to his phone; he always liked collecting moments where his family looked happy. For some of the wealthiest people in the city, he couldn't help but feel there weren't many moments of pure joy for them. They were all so busy, or stressed, or trying to prove themselves.

But saving the photo just reminded him of the girl again, and he swiped to the photos of her work he had taken.

Again, he had no idea why he had taken those. He had paid for a cleaning company to come spray-blast the walls and had been there when they arrived. But as they had set up their equipment, he'd been compelled to document at least *something* of her work before it was erased from reality entirely.

He looked at the photo again, seeing a story there even though it was only half finished. There was so much character to the figure that she had finished, he wondered what it would have looked like if she had a chance to complete whatever she was going for.

An alert sounded from his desktop and he shook his head, setting his phone face down on his office desk. He was in the middle of overlooking the negotiations they were entering into with a different health insurance company. The McLintoc Miller Ranch was considering switching to a new company that would save them considerable money, but he wanted to make sure the change was worth all the headaches it would cause.

He had no doubt that several of the workers would be miffed about it. They would complain about having to change primary care physicians and who knew what else. But there wouldn't be any decrease in care, supposedly, and there could potentially be a lower deductible, but Solomon wanted to triple check that that was the case before they moved any farther forward.

Of course, Dad was irritated with that, but there were some things that Dad would have to deal with. Making sure that the workers wouldn't be losing quality of care for a few thousand was absolutely worth it.

But try as he might to return his attention to the files in front of him on his computer, he couldn't concentrate. He found himself reading the same words over and over again ad nauseam.

Well, that wasn't helping him at all, and he needed his full mind if he was going to go over something so important. So instead, he headed over to his email where there would probably be enough busywork to get himself back on track mentally.

But instead, one of the first things he saw was something from his younger brother. Clicking on it, he saw it was a link to an article about the event that he had just attended at the megachurch.

It was fairly banal, as such things went, but embedded toward the end of it in the "related links" section, he saw a headline for "Rising Graffiti in Affluent Parts of City."

Huh, that definitely seemed relevant to everything that was happening.

Before he thought better of it, he was clicking on the link and waiting for it to load. Although he had stopped her from finishing her mural, he could definitely recognize her style on three distinct pieces. All of them were chock full of political or religious iconography, and he could see the messages she was trying to get across. One of them was two rich, celebrity looking busts of a man and a woman dripping in jewels while several people in rags looked up at them in awe. There was a more abstract one of a post on social media about "thoughts and prayers" with hundreds of likes while a wounded man lay bleeding out on the ground below it. The other one was just a young girl, but several parts of her body had arrows pointing to them and labels as to how they were deemed dangerous or inappropriate to society.

It was an awful lot to get across in graffiti, and yet she did. And for some reason, those messages—as clear as they were—irritated him to no end.

Why? That didn't make sense. He could listen to political rhetoric from every side of the aisle for hours with a banal smile and agreeable expression. But her art didn't allow for that. They made him feel...

Guilty.

And he didn't like that feeling at all.

He hadn't done anything wrong. He couldn't help that he was born a Miller. He couldn't help that his father was incredibly rich and that he himself had a knack for growing their business.

And yet he felt somehow responsible for the discord in the images that he was seeing, and that disquieted him.

He ended up staring at them for far too long, thinking about why he was being affected by something as simple as street art, and what that meant, when slowly a pattern began to float up from the data he was absorbing.

An idea coming to him, he started plugging the addresses into a map until he had them all marked with red clusters. Sure enough, his hunch was spot on, and all three of the ones he recognized—and several he didn't—were all within a mile and a half of a local park, the one that had all the water and cool-down areas for when the heat was really scorching. It had been a big deal on the news when that project had been launched, and cases of heatstroke among children and runners had gone down considerably.

But, as a result, during the few months of cooler weather, those areas generally went unused by a majority of the public and had become a sort of hang out for teens and ne'er-do-wells. The girl and whoever else was tagging were probably using that space as a meetup area, or at least a planning one. Nothing else made sense.

A knock sounded on his door. He looked up to see Salvatore, his second-to-youngest brother who had somehow outgrown all of them. While it was pretty clear that Solomon had inherited the business savvy, Sal had inherited all of the brawn. Standing at six foot five, he was tall even for a Miller, and his biceps were about as big as his head. While Solomon liked working out—it was the one area where he felt like he could properly vent stress—his brother practically lived in the gym sometimes.

Then again, Solomon supposed that came with the territory of having four older brothers. There wasn't exactly a ton of responsibility laying around for Sal, even though he was always clearly chomping at the bit, hoping to be helpful, to grab onto some sort of accomplishment and recognition. He wasn't like Simon, the youngest of their brood, who was off at college and had already realized that there wasn't much around for the baby of the family to do.

Solomon might have felt bad for his little brother if he wasn't ready to pull his hair out most of the time at growing the McLintoc Miller empire.

"What's going on in here? I was just down in the kitchens with Mrs. Hernandez, and she says that you haven't asked for lunch in days. You forgetting to eat again?"

Oh... had he eaten? He couldn't remember. It didn't seem important. Between the negotiations, dealing with a charity banquet that was courting his Dad as a primary speaker, Samuel leaving, and the girl, he felt like his brain was running on empty.

"I'll eat soon. I've just been busy."

"Yeah, I can tell as much. Your desk always gets messy when you're in the weeds."

"...in the weeds?"

"It's something Mrs. Hernandez taught me from her daughter. You know she's working two waitressing jobs while going to college full time? Mrs. Hernandez is helping her as best she can, but you know, being our housekeeper only pays so much."

"We pay well above the minimum average for the city," Solomon said, only half-listening. Mrs. Hernandez had been a staple in their house since he was fifteen. She was part of their staff of ten and her duties usually involved food and recreation. She was nice, professional and polite, which was all that really mattered to Solomon.

"I just think it's kind of weird, isn't it? She and her daughter are busting their butts when we could just like... probably cover her entire education without even blinking an eye. Literal chump change to us. But we don't. You ever think about that?"

Solomon finally *really* looked at his twenty-two-year-old brother. "If we pay for her college education, then we'd have to pay for all of our employees."

"Yeah," he nodded, rubbing his chin. "You know, I don't pay attention to a lot of the money stuff, but would that even be unaffordable for us?"

Solomon didn't know where all of his questions were

coming from. "What's going on? You suddenly guilty about how hard our family has worked?"

"Nah," he shrugged easily. "Just sometimes I think of these questions and I can't answer them. Like, if folks are poor, they should just work harder. But Mrs. Hernandez and her daughter work as hard as anyone I know, but they always seem so broke. And you know I can't ask Dad any of this stuff."

No, no he most certainly couldn't. Anyone who dared suggest that maybe they could be a little more generous, might pay a "living wage" or stop trying to find the most cost-saving insurance benefits would be met with an hour or two rant about people expecting handouts, relying on welfare, and needing to pull themselves up by their bootstraps.

Solomon had used to agree with his dad wholeheartedly. But since he had learned more about economics, and budgeting, and how money worked in general, he wasn't so sure anymore.

Much of how their system was built involved keeping the poor, poor and the wealthy, wealthy. Maximizing profits and valuing money above human life. It was all sticky and messy and always made for a sleepless night.

"Anyway, what's going on? You seem a little rattled."

Solomon thought about brushing him off. But considering that his brother was always looking for a way to help, maybe there was a way to get himself settled and also give Sal something to do.

"Honestly, I've got this... vandal on my mind. They tagged that megachurch we sponsored the refurbishment of and some other places too." He didn't know why he didn't mention that she was a female right off the bat. Maybe because he didn't want his brother to assume things. Maybe he was embarrassed by being outrun by a young woman. "I think I might have found where they and their gang are all meeting up to coordinate things, but I'm not sure."

"Huh, really? That actually sounds interesting for once. I thought you mostly dealt with all that egghead stuff up here."

"Egghead stuff?"

"Yeah, you know. Percentages, taxes and property values. Business ventures. Politics. All of that not-fun stuff."

"You know, life isn't meant to be fun all the time."

"I know. I sit through our occasional family dinners just like the rest of you."

That startled a laugh from Solomon, and he found his mind quickly making itself up. "What do you say? Want to help your egghead brother try to confront these vandals? See if we can find them in the park?"

"You realize there's almost no chance of you catching them there, right?"

"I know. But I've got a hunch."

Sal shrugged, flashing one of his easy smiles. "Why not? You know I've got nothing better to do."

Grinning himself, Solomon stood and grabbed his jacket. "All right then, let's go."

5

———————

Frenchie

On her sketchpad, she drew the water of the artificial pond and all the animals surrounding it, deep into the zone as her hand moved across the paper. She shaded in with charcoal, her moldable eraser in her other hand, turning it over with her fingers.

Frenchie was well aware that some people would look dubiously at her owning art supplies when she was so hard up, but they were people who didn't really understand what it was like to be broke. They didn't get that, occasionally, she would get a nice present for her birthday or Christmas from a charity or a friend who wasn't strapped for cash. They didn't get that lost and founds were often a treasure trove for colored pencils and pens. They didn't understand that sometimes, spending the last three dollars on a good charcoal was worth all the free therapy she would get from it.

Because that was what creation really was. A sort of therapy. She always found it calming to sketch water and nature scenes. Soothing, making her feel connected to the world instead of adjacent to it. It was a balm to her anxiety, which sometimes felt so all-consuming that her mind was going to turn itself inside out.

Appreciating the beauty of the world, all the wonderful, warm and happy things in it was the only medicine she could really afford, and she certainly wasn't going to take it for granted. Her plight could be a lot worse. She could be blind, deaf, unable to walk. So she would celebrate what she had, even if it made some folks give her the side eye.

She munched on the last of her bagels as she listened to her MP3 player, her head bopping along. She was actually having a pretty good day. Her belly was full of a hot meal she'd scored earlier plus her bagel snack, and she had a gig lined up for the weekend. It wasn't going to pay a ton, but seventy dollars could go a long way for her. Especially if she drew it out with some soup kitchen meals and the like.

It was nice. She had almost forgotten what nice felt like. If things kept going good, she might have enough money to settle herself, make it so that she didn't have to hop around all the time, accepting whatever odd jobs she could get here and there.

Humming to herself, she had no idea how long she stayed there until she eventually went to grab her always-present thermos, only to find that it was empty.

Well, that wouldn't do at all.

Packing up her stuff to make sure that no one stole it, she put her backpack on and headed to the water fountain that was just a bit away. It was one of the good ones, with a special spot for refilling water bottles and a little ticker that said how many plastic containers it had saved people from throwing away. The water would be pretty tasty, unlike some of the tin-tasting older ones.

It was a quick process, and yet while she was standing there, she swore that she felt eyes on her. It was a disquieting feeling, and one that she had long since learned not to ignore.

Looking up, she let her gaze scope the horizon, looking for any threat. That was when she spotted *him*, and her blood ran cold.

It was the man that had chased her for blocks from the church, ruining her tag and stealing her hoody. It was the reason she had been so cold of late and expended so much energy on finding a nice coat.

Horror filled her, the kind of all-consuming, blood rushing, stomach curdling fear, and the next thing she knew, she was running for her life.

Why was the man there again? And how did he know that she would be in the park? It was nowhere near the megachurch, and it wasn't like those upper echelon folks would ever visit such a low-income part of the city anyway, one that was reliant on charity and public funding.

Did he want to hurt her? He had to, why else would he have tracked her down? She had barely gotten away when he had chased her, and she had felt how strong he was when he grabbed her hoody. If he wanted to, he could hurt her pretty badly. Maybe even kill her. Frenchie had seen what happened to her friends when someone who had violence in mind got a hold of them. She didn't want to end up like that. She was only twenty-three, she didn't want to *end* at all!

She went for one of the playgrounds, one of the easiest ways to dodge and hide. While the man was faster and no doubt stronger than her, his weight would work to his disadvantage. He wouldn't be able to dodge, dive, and juke like she could with a full range of equipment at her disposal.

She rushed there, shooting between a thicket of bushes that separated one of the calm areas where the older folks liked to sit from the louder, children's areas. She popped up quickly, looking over her shoulder to see that it looked like she had lost him for at least a few seconds.

Perfect. It would be just enough to give her a head start. Maybe she could—

Her thoughts cut off as she slammed right into what felt like a wall. She bounced backward, wondering when they had constructed a wall without her knowing, only to look up and see an absolute giant of a man.

She stared up at him, her terror intensifying that much further. She didn't know if she ever saw someone so *big*, and suddenly she was absolutely sure that she was about to be murdered.

No, no, *no*. It couldn't happen like this. She scuttled backward, on her butt, when she heard someone emerge from the bushes behind her.

She was trapped. Pinned between the two. A giant and a chaser, both of them too big for her. Would anyone miss her if she was gone? Her friends wouldn't report her missing to the police. They knew better than to waste their time with that. The cops didn't care if someone like her was gone. They'd probably blame her or say that she was just another junkie that got too high.

Scrambling for her pack, she thrust her hand in the front pouch, where she kept her defense items. Fingers wrapping around a smooth cylinder, she yanked it out and aimed it at the man in front of her, fighting to her feet.

She managed to backpedal enough so that they were in a

sort of triangle, a can of wasp-spray in her hand. It wasn't pepper spray, but it would sting and blind just as badly without getting her jailtime.

"Stay away from me!" she cried, pitching her voice higher. "I'll scream!"

No, she wouldn't. She wasn't stupid enough not to know what would happen if people stumbled across someone who looked like her in a tussle with two well-dressed men who had political connections, judging by the church one of them had chased her from.

They slowed at that, both holding their hands up. That was good. They needed to understand that she would put up a fight. She wouldn't come quietly. She would kick and struggle. She would make them *hurt*.

"Whoa, calm down there," the giant one said, his tone more than a bit patronizing. It was hard not to flinch as he spoke. The man had to be over six and a half feet, and his arms were nearly the size of her waist. He could probably rip her in two if he wanted.

"Calm *down*?" she repeated incredulously, aiming the can first at one of them, then the other. Her movements were jerky, panicked. Adrenaline was pumping through her something fierce, and she was nearly dizzy from it. "Why should I calm down when you're following me? *Why* are you following me!?"

The two of them exchanged looks like they had no idea why she was so frightened. How could they not know? They had no right to look so mystified.

"You defaced my family's property," the one who had chased her first said slowly, as if he was just coming up with the reasoning that moment.

"Your... family?" That brought up a slew of questions inside of her head. If his family somehow owned a megachurch... she shuddered. If they had that kind of money and power, she didn't want to think about what they could get away with. She'd heard far too many horror stories about folks like her ending up at the bottom of rivers or landfills.

"Yes. We partially own the church and a few other properties you've tagged."

Wait... a few other properties?

Despite how fast her mind was moving, it took her several seconds to put the pieces together. She was always specific in the places she targeted, going for ones owned by the elite of the elite. If she remembered right, the last handful had been owned by a disgustingly rich family that had a sort of mega-ranch outside of the very city that they profited from.

Oh.

Oh *no*.

Admittedly, Frenchie had gotten herself into bad situations plenty of times, but she began to wonder if she had just gotten herself into the worst one she'd ever been in.

"W-what do you want?" She hated how her voice trembled. She was strong, she liked being known as strong, but she couldn't help how rattled she was in the moment.

Yeah, she knew technically defacing public property was wrong, but wasn't abusing the poor and hoarding wealth like dragons wrong too? Sometimes she burned with so much anger at how things worked that painting those scenes felt like the only way she was heard. Kind of like Robin Hood, but less useful.

"Are you going to take me to jail?" she continued. While the warmth and the three solid meals were tempting, she didn't want to end up there. She knew she wouldn't last; that it would chew her up and spit her out, and that a criminal record would make her ever getting back on the straight and narrow that much more difficult.

"What? Jail?" He seemed confused, which made no sense to her. "No." He licked his lips, and he might have been handsome, but she was still too scared to really take inventory of it. "I just... I just wanted to confront you."

That couldn't be true. Surely... surely that was too easy. He didn't track her down and chase her just to talk it out? That wasn't how the world worked. She was sure of it.

"Well consider me confronted. Well and truly. Can I go now?"

"I want you to promise you won't tag any more places."

That... that couldn't be it. "Sure," she snorted. Whatever he wanted to hear. She'd promise to walk on the moon if it meant she could get away.

His eyes flitted to the taller one uncertainly, and the motion made her want to throttle him. How dare he chase her down and then not even know what to do! She knew she was benefiting from it, but it certainly made her head and stomach twist around themselves.

But instead of arguing with her, or saying that "sure" wasn't enough, he stepped to the side to let her go.

Huh.

That was not what she expected.

Still suspecting that there was a trap, she carefully moved past them. She was so tense she swore she might just burst then and there, but she managed to make it several steps away.

She didn't know what emboldened her when she felt so terrified, but the next thing she knew, she was turning slightly to look back at them.

"Hey, do you have the hoody you stole from me? Because it's cold."

That seemed to baffle him even more, and she was getting tired of that look on his face.

"You don't have another one to use?"

She rolled her eyes at that. Of course, he didn't understand. Her hoody, with its wonderful fleece lining, was probably in a trashcan somewhere. Oh well. She supposed she should be grateful that he wasn't trying to citizen arrest her and just get the hell out of dodge.

She trotted off, murmuring to herself how rich people were the worst.

6

———————

Solomon

"I'm just saying, you didn't even try to threaten the girl with any repercussions. Seems like an awful long drive to not even bring up consequences for vandalism."

Solomon pulled himself from his thoughts but kept his eyes on the road as his younger brother spoke. Neither of them had said much of anything since their encounter, even though he could tell that Sal was bristling from the effort.

It wasn't that Solomon had intended for things to work out the way they had, but when they had finally managed to get the girl between them, her reaction of utter terror had knocked him sideways.

Sure, he expected her to be upset—as criminals always were when they were caught. He expected her to be mad. Angry. Violent. But none of that had been on her face when she'd held up that spray can and squeaked at them to stop.

No, it had been fear there. Raw terror. The kind of utterly panicked look that people in horror movies wore when they were being chased down by a killer. In fact, her whole body seemed like it was locked in a state of fear, her hand shaking, her chest rising and falling rapidly while her voice was trembling.

It was nothing like the defiant girl who had flipped him off in the dark, and her reaction had given him pause. Made him stop for a moment and imagine what things were like through her eyes.

She asked what he wanted like he was some kind of thug there to hurt her. He realized that, for all she knew, he was. But then she was asking about jail too, and suddenly, he didn't understand why he was there at all or what he had hoped. He was so sure that there was no chance of running into the girl, that he hadn't stopped and thought about what would happen if they *did*.

And it had seemed like they were going to fail at first. They'd searched all of the cool-down structures and that entire area of the park and come up only with trash. If it hadn't been for Sal needing to take a wiz and insisting on using the nicer, refurbished bathrooms toward the center of the park, he never would have spotted her at all.

He'd been so shocked at seeing her in the daylight that he'd just stood there for a moment, taking her in. She was swaying slightly, her head rhythmically moving to a beat he couldn't hear. She had a backpack on, but her outfit wasn't appropriate for the weather. She was wearing tattered jean shorts with worn leggings under them and a long flannel. That was it. He was sure that she was cold, and yet she was standing there, filling up a thermos like nothing was amiss.

Her figure was womanly, of that there was no doubt, but

there was a wavering sort of thinness to her, like she was just getting over being sick or had gone through a rough patch. Solomon knew that women came in all sizes, but there was something about her frame, her posture, that spoke of it being smaller than it would prefer. He saw it on his mom when her sister had passed away after a long struggle with cancer. He saw it on Sterling when his twin, Silas, had gotten into a car accident when they were younger and spent months in recovery.

His hands itched, like he had wanted to do something about it, but instead he'd just chased her.

In retrospect, that was probably dumb.

"Hello, earth to Solomon."

Oh right, his brother had been speaking to him.

"She looked scared enough already."

"Hah, you're not kidding about that. You would'a thought we were coming at her with machetes with the way she reacted. Jeez."

Solomon nodded, but his gaze flicked to the hoody in the backseat of the car. Her last words lingered with him, so incongruous to the rest of their conversation, and he found himself turning it this way and that again.

"I wonder why it's so significant to her?"

"Huh? What is?"

"The hoody," he said, gesturing to the back and taking his eyes off the rearview mirror to focus on the road.

"Well, it's probably her only one."

No, that didn't make sense at all. "What kind of person only has one jacket?" It wasn't even a good one. It was threadbare with ragged patches on the elbows. There were stains on it and more than a couple of rips. He'd checked the inside of it too when he'd first gotten into his truck on that fateful night, hoping for some sort of clue for who the mystery girl was, but all he'd found was worn, scratchy fleece.

He was surprised when his brother laughed, joshing him on the arm. "For being so smart, you sure can be dense sometimes. The girl only has one because she's almost definitely homeless."

Solomon's eyes shot wide and his stomach did a funny sort of acrobatic flip. *Homeless?* But weren't homeless people supposed to be druggies and alcoholics or crazies? People who, basically, *deserved* it? It didn't make any sense for her to be homeless.

"How do you know that?"

"The signs were all there. Out in a public park in the middle of the day. No coat and wanted her hoody back. A real industrial backpack that's definitely seen things. Her MP3 player is super old, she didn't seem to have a phone, and her headphones were cheap ones from a gas station. Instead of having a trendy water bottle with a filter, she had an old soup thermos, like the kind you'd pack in a kid's lunch if you were a parent who did that kind of thing."

Solomon just blinked at his brother, surprised again by Sal in less than two minutes. "You noticed all that while coming out of the bathroom?"

"Well, yeah, if I'm going to chase down a skinny little girl, I want to know why."

"Little girl? She's probably your age."

"Maybe. Hard to tell sometimes. But it was clear that she could use a good meal and she wasn't just rocking a model look for funsies. I bet if she was fueled up, neither of us could have caught her."

Solomon nodded absently, his mind still running a thousand miles a minute at the revelation. *Homeless!?*

"Anyways, she's probably some girl with daddy issues who got into the system. From what I've read, they almost always end up on the streets."

"Really?" Solomon asked, licking his lips. It was an anxious habit of his, and at the moment, he was definitely feeling anxious. "What exactly have you been reading lately?"

"Honestly, everything. I'm not just a muscle head, you know. I figured with Samuel basically abandoning the family for Aunt Annie and Uncle Douglas, that maybe I shouldn't take everything for granted and should try to figure out some stuff for myself."

"Admirable."

"Really? Thanks. I like keeping myself informed."

"Uh-huh."

He was glad his brother was spreading his wings, but he couldn't concentrate on that. No, all he could think about was the girl and the fact that she might have no home.

What did she do at night? And if he had her jacket, what would she do when it got colder? Was she safe? Did she have a place to rest her head where she didn't have to worry about someone laying their hands on her? What did she eat? Was he wrong, and she was just naturally slender, or were those collar bones sticking out too much because she didn't have enough to eat...

His thoughts whirled around him, consuming most of his thinking that wasn't dedicated to driving the car. He had no idea what to think or any way to know if his brother was right. But suddenly, none of it sat very well with him.

So much for their little trip giving him some relief.

7

Frenchie

"Get out!"

Frenchie woke up with a jolt, her mouth blurting out words even when her vision was still hazy from sleep. She bared the box cutter she always kept on herself when she slept, sure that someone was invading her cozy little hiding place.

And someone was, but thankfully it was just a stray cat, and double thankfully one of the kitties that actually liked her and wasn't completely covered in fleas.

"Hey there, little guy," she said, laughing a bit giddily. She reached out, waiting for him to sniff her fingers and welcome her touch. She loved all the little strays and ferals that wandered around the area—even if most of them had fleas. She couldn't feed them very often, as usually her food consisted of carbs or canned goods. But on the special occasion where she could score meat, she always tried to share with the sweet little guys.

"You scared the pants off me, you know that?"

Technically that wasn't true. She didn't own any pants. She had her shorts, two pairs of leggings—one of which she was wearing—and a skirt. That was the grand total of her bottoms. She was hoping that she could manage to get some sweats before winter set in, but the clothing charities around the area seemed unusually strapped for the time of year.

The cat let out a soft trill, coming up alongside her to sidle along her arm as a sign that she could proceed with the petting. He was a particular tomcat, one who only liked to be stroked on the top of his head, his cheeks, and the base of his tail, but he was a good boy. And a good hunter too, judging by the fact that he wasn't entirely skin and bones. It made her feel a bit less guilty by how rarely she had treats to share. Especially since his warm little body gave her perpetually cold and chapped hands plenty of heat to leech off of.

She was tempted to curl up with him for a while and just stay in her little hiding spot; it was a good one after all—one that she'd had for a while—but she knew she needed to get up and go about her day. It was getting too cold to laze about for long, and she hadn't eaten at all the previous day.

And so, she went about putting on both of the tops that she owned and heading out into the cold air. It would warm up once the sun got higher in the sky and did its thing, but she really needed to go and get a jacket. She was tempted to nick one from a store, but she heard that the forecast was calling for mid-forties, and that meant all of the loss prevention personnel at the stores were going to be on high alert for winter apparel thefts.

She didn't know how homeless people did it in really cold

places, such as the East coast. She was pretty sure she would have long since kicked the bucket if she didn't happen to have ended up homeless someplace warm. Sure, Texas could get to below freezing occasionally in the dead of winter, but she still had time before she had to worry about that.

...not a lot of time. But time, nonetheless.

Frenchie rubbed her arms as she headed toward the block to get her stale bagels. Her mouth watered at the idea of food, but her thoughts shot in a different direction, back toward tastes and memories from before the streets had been her home.

She remembered the luxuries of lox. And cream cheese. Honestly, just protein in general. She remembered what it was like to know that she probably was going to have food and that she had a bed every night. The only issue was that bed, that shelter, that food, came with unspoken conditions that she wouldn't give in to. Given the choice, she'd picked the best option.

But goodness, what she wouldn't do for a smoked salmon bagel.

She didn't ask for that, of course, and wasn't given one. She was pleased, however, to see that there were several everything bagels along with some sesame and poppy seed ones. Although she hated how they felt against her teeth, all those extra bits would be good protein and calories that would help her stretch them out longer. If only she could get something high in iron, then she might actually feel less like she was going to fall over.

There was always one of the shelters. She knew that, but with winter temperatures upon them, it was hard to find a space in one. And even if she did, she was a bit nervous about those two men being there.

Funny, she had avoided shelters at first because she didn't want to be found, and she was afraid of being reported as both a runaway and minor. By the time she had aged out of it ever being a problem, it had just become so much of a habit that half the time she forgot that they existed. But now that she'd been hunted down and somehow caught at one of her hangouts, she found herself sinking into that old paranoia again.

Which was silly. She was twenty-three. Her "father" had no doubt long since forgotten about her, and her mother was probably still relieved at her absence. She'd been on the streets since she was sixteen, and after six years, she didn't really have much of an excuse for being so scared of being caught.

And yet she was.

It had been a week since that chase in the park, and she always felt like those two men were going to pop out from behind her at any moment. Put her in jail or ship her back to the place that never was home. And even though the logical part of herself knew that wasn't likely, that was still what her brain told her all the time.

She needed money. The beginning of winter was the worst. When the holidays were too far away to call upon all the charity and goodwill that was supposed to be in the air, and all the gigs that came from the spring and summer turned to mist. Panhandling wasn't something she wanted to do, as there were fewer people outside, and those that were around generally wanted to get wherever they were going as fast as they could.

She needed to go to the park and see if she could sell some caricatures before it got too cold for people to sit still for them. Once it did, the only time she could do that was around the holidays, when people got particularly festive and romantic.

Ugh. Romance. Talk about a luxury for the rich. The few street kids she knew that had coupled up were only together for survival's sake. Now that she was older, most of the homeless her age were too tired, too run down, and too suspicious for anything remotely like dating. She couldn't even remember the last time she had seen a movie in the theater or sat in an actual restaurant. Plus, dating required some measure of trust. The only thing she ever trusted was money in her hand.

...which she had none of at the moment. The last of hers being spent on heat packets to keep her hands and feet warm during the longer and longer nights.

She *really* needed to earn some cash soon, and fast.

Wrinkling her nose, she changed directions and headed toward the park. Her heartbeat was kicking up and her stomach was twisting at the possibility of being cornered by those two men. Surely, they had to have something else in mind for her. Who chased her down twice and then let her go with a verbal warning? It didn't make any sense. That wasn't how the world worked.

Naturally, when she finally arrived at the park and scoped out the best spot, she was feeling more than a little nervous. She forced herself to settle down, however, because no one would sit for a caricature if they thought she was a tweaker, even though she wasn't on drugs and never would be.

Easier said than done, but somehow, she managed, and as the hours passed, she got a total of three people to sit for her. It wasn't going to break anyone's bank, but the fifteen dollars in her pocket sure was nice. That would get her some fast food somewhere, a couple more of those insta-hot packs and then five dollars to save for if she was really desperate for transportation, food, or shelter.

She could only stay out for so long, however, and soon the light became too scant while her fingers grew too cold. She began to pack up her things when a shadow fell across her.

Frenchie stiffened, an entirely new type of cold shooting through her, and she turned to see it was *him*. The guy. She stared at him, utterly shocked despite the fact that her paranoia had been so sure that he would show up, and she tensed to bolt out of there like a bat out of hell.

But as she jumped to her feet, spilling the contents of her bag everywhere, she noticed something. He wasn't coming toward her. He wasn't even moving. He just had one hand stretched out, a familiar bit of fabric hanging from it.

...her jacket?

She swallowed hard, licking her lips and looking from her fleece-lined hoody back to him. "Are you serious right now?" she heard herself ask. It was a trick. It had to be a trick. There was no way he tracked her down a second time just to return a piece of clothing to her.

"It's yours. It's only right that I return it. I'm not a thief."

She wasn't sure if he was implying that *she* was a thief, but she didn't quite care. Reaching out tentatively, she kept her muscles tensed in case he tried to pull something. But then her hoody was in her hands—did he *wash* it!?—and she was taking a step back without him having even moved so much as an inch.

"Uh, well, thanks, I guess. For returning it."

"Of course."

One of the reasons Frenchie had survived so long was because she could read people real well. And she could have been mistaken, but she was pretty sure that the guy was feeling just as awkward as she did—which was entirely his own fault.

"All right, I gotta go."

"Right, right. It's getting dark. I'm sure you have to get home."

Home, right. She just gave him a vague shrug and bent to

shove her things back into her bag. She was surprised when she stood and found the man still there, watching her nervously.

Normally, if any man kept his eyes on her for that long, she would assume he was after something. But the guy in front of her didn't seem lecherous, or even appreciative. Just mostly… weird.

She hoped he wasn't one of those serial killers. Weren't they usually rich white guys though? She couldn't remember if that was the case or if that was white-collar crime. Ugh, she needed to find a way to get a library card again so she could research these things. The old library had closed, and she was required to get a new one but didn't have an address to do so.

"Hey, are you hungry?" he asked.

Well that was just about the last thing that she had expected, so she stared at him a moment before realizing that she should probably answer one way or another. The truth would probably be all right, especially since he brought her the jacket back.

"Yeah, I'm always hungry."

"You want to go get something?"

Huh, so he was one of those. Weird, because his face read as anything but attracted to her. No, he was looking at her more like he was afraid she would shoot him rather than someone to rent for the night.

"I'm not for sale," she answered firmly. She'd long since learned that trying to let them down easy or being sweet didn't do the trick. Sure, some guys got mad about it, but they rarely caused a scene beyond calling her things she'd heard plenty of times before.

But to her surprise, the man just turned a bright shade of

red. "W-what?! No, not like that. I just—" He let out a breath and ran his hand through his hair.

She just noticed how thick it was, slicked slightly back with a product that probably cost three times more than anything that she owned.

He started talking again. "There's a diner around that I wanted to try, but I don't like eating alone. It's depressing."

Well... that actually made sense. She remembered when she was younger that she and her friends went everywhere together, including the bathroom. On the few occasions since that she'd had enough money to eat, she'd always tried to bring one of her allies on the streets with her.

But then again, it could just be another trick. It was amazing the lengths that some people would go through to hurt other people, and she wasn't about to fall for the adult equivalent of getting into a windowless van marked "free candy."

"Will I need to get into your truck to get there?"

Because that was a hard no. No matter how nice a warm meal from anywhere sounded, it wouldn't be worth her life. She knew what happened to girls like her when they lowered their guards, and she had no desire to end up like one of those stories on the news.

Her stomach twisted at the thought. The worst thing about those stories, beyond that some innocent woman had lost her life while fighting to survive, was that they were a form of entertainment for so many. A salacious and shocking tale to talk about at the office, maybe feel guilty about for a few minutes, but then long forgotten by the end of the day. No one *really* cared.

"Actually, I thought we would walk. It's close by, along the main road. Not a ton of traffic, but enough."

She didn't have to ask him what he meant by enough and he didn't have to clarify. There would be enough people so she wouldn't be alone, wouldn't be put into a vulnerable position. It made her feel a little strange that he had clearly given thought to how she might feel, and she couldn't tell if that was a bad or good thing.

Still suspicious, she found herself slowly nodding. A free meal did sound mighty nice.

8

Solomon

*W*hat was he doing?

He didn't know, and no answers came to that question as he stared at the young woman sitting across the booth from him. He felt strangely detached from his body, like it had gone and made a bunch of decisions without his input.

He hadn't planned on asking her to eat. In fact, he hadn't even planned on returning the clothing to her. But after it had sat in his truck for a couple of days, he finally brought it inside, intending to throw it away. If the girl was so concerned about it, she shouldn't have been defacing public property.

But something had stopped him from tossing it in the trash, and instead he just set it to the side. The last thing he expected was for it to get picked up by one of the housekeepers when he was busy, or for it to be washed and left out on the counter with a sticky note that she wasn't sure who it belonged to.

After that, he couldn't help but feel like it was a sign from God that he needed to give it back to her. He didn't believe Sal's guess that the girl was homeless, and yet the idea niggled at the back of his mind.

Because if she was, and she died because he had her hoody, did that make him a murderer?

But she couldn't be homeless. She wasn't one of *those* types; he could tell just by looking at her. Sure, she was clearly a bit entitled and mischievous, tagging public places as she was, but she wasn't like the dirty people he saw on the side of the road with signs begging for help.

And yet he had ended up in the park anyway, looking for her. And when she didn't show up, he'd looked again two days later. And the next day. He was just about to chalk the whole thing up as a silly lark when he spotted her, all curled on herself while she drew.

And now he was sitting across from her at a diner, able to look at her in more detail.

...she was in pretty rough shape. Her hands were chapped and calloused, with little scabs around her cuticles that spoke of hangnails. There were holes in the leggings she wore under her shorts, and he could see a bruise on one of her shins. Her hair was messy like she hadn't brushed it in a day or two and once again, he was struck by the thought that she looked thinner than she was meant to be.

He swallowed, that strange feeling rising in him again as she gripped the coffee cup in front of her, her eyes closed and a faint smile about her lips as if she was soaking up the warmth into her body. And considering her state, she could be. Almost as soon as they'd begun to walk, she'd slipped her hoody over her head, doing a strange sort of maneuvering to get her back-pack off then back on without stopping.

"So, what am I having?"

He started, thinking that he had been caught staring, but he realized the strange woman's eyes were looking down at the menu. How old was she? It was hard to tell. In some ways she seemed so small, so youthful, and in others she seemed older. Wearier.

"Whatever you want," he said with a shrug, even though she couldn't see the movement. He was reminded of the words she had said to him when he asked if she was hungry, the steel in her eyes as she told him she wasn't selling herself. He hadn't meant to imply that at all, but now he was beginning to wonder if he'd managed to dispel her belief that he was angling to get something out of her dining with him.

Because he really wasn't. He wasn't even sure *why* he had asked her, but he knew it wasn't that.

"Hi, y'all! It's getting chilly out there, isn't it? What can I get for you?"

He looked up, startled. He had almost forgotten that they were in a diner, and of course, a server would be coming to take their order.

"It is," he tried to answer smoothly. "I'll have the strip steak along with the biscuits in gravy. Extra gravy."

"And to drink, love?"

Oh. He had forgotten that, hadn't he? "Just a water. No lemon."

"Sounds like a plan. And you, darling?"

The young woman's gaze flicked to Solomon's, as if she was trying to decide if he was full of it or not. "I'll have your T-bone steak, all the fixin's on it, a baked potato, all the fixin's with extra sour. I'd like a side of bacon, your biscuits and gravy, definitely a large side of eggs. And *oh!* Definitely your eggs Benedict."

She never broke her stare with Solomon, and he got the feeling that she was challenging him for daring to say she could have whatever she liked. But to be honest, it was difficult for him not to laugh. He found it strangely amusing, even though he was pretty sure that she was specifically trying to annoy him.

"You sure that you can eat all of that, sugar?" the waitress said with a genial tone.

"Oh, I'm sure I can manage."

"Besides," Solomon said, cutting in smoothly, "we heard the food here is so good, can you blame her for wanting some leftovers?"

"Huh, well I guess not. Well, I'll put that in for you and get your drinks. Do you know what you'd like to drink, darling?"

"I'll take the largest sweet tea you have and a water too, no lemon."

"All righty then, I'll be back soon with the drinks."

The woman walked off, leaving Solomon and the girl alone again.

He supposed that he should stop mentally calling her "girl," "woman," and "young woman," but he didn't know her name, and it seemed rude to ask just out of the blue. Then again, there wasn't any etiquette for speaking to a strange vandal who liked defacing churches and other nice buildings.

"So, my name's Solomon," he said awkwardly. He wasn't used to not knowing what to do or say. Part of his skill in helping his father's business was how good he was at reading and schmoozing with the right people, but when it came to the young woman in front of him, he felt like he was on entirely different ground.

"That your real name?"

He blinked at her. "Yeah, why wouldn't it be?" His name was like a brand; it carried a certain amount of trust and dependability to it. Why would he deny it?

"You really don't know how the real world works, do you?"

"And you do?"

"Aye, I got an idea." She crossed her arms and sat back.

Her hazel eyes were narrowed, and he felt like he was being studied.

"Usually this is the part where you tell me your name."

"Oh, is it?"

She was testing him again, challenging him. But if there was one thing Solomon usually was, it was patient. So, he sat there, returning her stare, as if sitting in complete silence was perfectly natural.

"Frenchie," she said finally. It seemed like whole minutes had passed before she caved.

"Come on, that's not your actual name."

"What, you don't like it?" she fluttered her lashes at him. "I think it's cute."

"You look more like an Emily to me."

She didn't at all, which was why he said that. She wrinkled her nose instantly and huffed. "Now why'd you have to go an' ruin a perfectly good meal?"

"How can you say it's good? We haven't even gotten the food yet."

"It's free, right? Automatically good."

He let out a small laugh at that. Despite the strange footing that they had gotten off on, he was pleased that they were able to banter back and forth easily. He was so used to people either trying to butter him up for favor, or being intimidated by the McLintoc name, that it was refreshing to talk to someone who clearly couldn't care less. In fact, she seemed much more interested in the coming food than him.

"Here are your drinks, lovelies. You need straws?"

"Yes, please," Frenchie answered, flashing the woman a blinding smile that surprised Solomon.

He hadn't seen her have such a happy expression since he had met her. If he hadn't witnessed it himself, he wouldn't have believed she was capable.

Frenchie continued, "I appreciate it."

"Of course, honey. Least I can do."

Then the waitress left, and Frenchie was right back to being a sour apple again. He found himself once more at a loss of what to say and let it fall quiet for far too long. A minute passed, then more. He could feel her foot bouncing under the table, her eyes shuttling up and down him repeatedly.

He wondered what she saw. If she was anyone else, he would say he had a good idea. Solomon was well aware that he was attractive to a majority of people. Or at least a majority of people around his parts. He had all the classic anatomy that ran in the Miller bloodline. He was tall, with thick hair, with sharp eyes and a solid bone structure. He was fairly fit.

"Anyways, you were saying?" Frenchie asked.

"Nothing important, it seems."

"Ah, something we can agree on."

Was it the politest thing to say? No, but she sent him a conspiratorial little smirk, and he couldn't help but grin a little too. Clearly the girl was a bit saucy, as his mom would say, but he didn't mind. She was forthright, and he quickly began to understand more about her.

But only a little bit.

Frenchie leaned forward and said, "So, do you make a habit of chasing down people multiple times just to offer them a meal? That's the most bizarre workout regimen I've ever heard of."

"No, not quite. I, uh, didn't plan this?"

She gave him another one of those *looks*. "Really? Not to be rude, but you seem like the type not to do anything unless he's got multiple reports on the possible risk and profit."

"Huh, for not being rude, that does sound an awful lot like an insult."

"Does it? Forgive me. My human skills are rusty."

"But not your painting skills, it seems."

His chest filled with pride when that startled a laugh out of her. Conversation wasn't a competition, but he couldn't help but feel like he was one step behind the young—*Frenchie.*

Huh, a peculiar sort of name for a peculiar sort of woman. As he watched her talk, watched her emote, he was struck by how pretty she was.

Wait, no, pretty wasn't the right word for it. Neither was beautiful. She looked like art, like someone had painstakingly created her with years of skill. She was dynamic and interesting, her hair a mess of colors, her cheekbones high, and her jaw strong. There was a catlike quality to her eyes, which made sense when it felt like sometimes her gaze was sizing him up. She was like those fantasy cards that his youngest cousin had been obsessed with when he was younger, an elf or a dryad, something deeply entrenched in nature and yet not a part of it at all.

She opened her mouth to respond and he noticed how full her lips were, despite them being a bit chapped and cracked in one corner. That meant something, didn't it? He vaguely recalled Mom saying her corners would split when she was low on something... calcium? Iron maybe?

But before she could answer or he could figure out her

dietary deficiency, the food came and wasn't *that* a sight to behold. With the help of another, their waitress laid their dishes out, filling pretty much the entire table. Frenchie just stared at all of the steaming food, as if she couldn't believe it was real, her hands hovering in the air like if she touched it, it would all disappear.

"Anything else I can get for y'all?"

"No, we're fine," Solomon answered after a beat when it was clear that the woman across from him was completely enraptured by the fare in front of her. "Thank you."

"Of course. I'll be by in a bit to check on ya."

She and the other server headed off, and Solomon picked up his utensils to get into his biscuits while they were still hot. Whenever he traveled, he always missed the gravy covered staple more than any other food. Something about it just spoke of home, and simpler times.

He was just about to bite into the first one when he noticed that Frenchie was still staring, her mouth moving wordlessly, her hands moving from plate to plate and yet never settling down.

Her expression was... something else. An intense mix of disbelief and wonder, bewilderment and amazement. Like she was looking at the most wonderful sight in the world and her excitement was overwhelming her.

He couldn't remember the last time that he had ever been that enthused about *anything.* And yet the woman in front of him was clearly having a kind of moment over less than a hundred dollars' worth of food.

"You should start with the biscuits," he advised ruefully, finally taking his own bite.

She glanced up at him with such a startled expression, like she had forgotten that he was there.

He explained, "If they sit there and soak up the gravy too much, then you miss the mix of textures."

She nodded wordlessly before finally, her hand went to her fork. Solomon tried to watch without looking like he was staring, wanting to see what her face would display once she actually tasted the comfort food.

He was not disappointed.

Her eyes went even wider, looking almost comical, and she just froze in place, the food in her slack mouth. It was a wonder that it didn't just slide right out and back onto her plate in a messy pile.

There was something about it that was just...adorable. Which it probably shouldn't have been, but her earnest enjoyment was just so nice. She wasn't putting on a show, wasn't faking. She was just genuinely happy about the food in front of her.

And he had provided that.

He wasn't sure what changed, but suddenly a switch was flipped, and she swallowed quickly before shoving several more bites right into her mouth in rapid succession. Her cheeks were chipmunked out as she chewed hastily then swallowed.

"Hey," he said, reaching out to rest his big hand over hers.

Instantly she jerked back, her grip on the fork changing as if she was going to stab him.

He pulled back quickly, hands up as if he was surrendering. "You just need to slow down. You're gonna make yourself sick."

She narrowed her eyes, as if she was about to snap at him not to tell her what to do, before slowly nodding. Returning to normal, she went over to her grits, took a single bite, before reaching to the side of the table and grabbing the salt shaker.

She upended it over her grits and he expected her to only shake it once or twice, but she just kept on shaking it as the crystals poured down from the shaker and formed a small mountain on top of the grits.

"Um, so you wanted salt with a side of grits then?"

"Huh? Oh. Right." She set it back on the table then stirred the mess up before hastily taking several bites.

She nodded along the whole time, as if giving the food her tacit approval, then finally moved onto the steak.

"*Protein*," she whispered to herself, almost reverently.

Solomon figured at that point he had been staring for far too long, and he went to his own food.

Their conversation pretty much stopped entirely as they both ate their meals. Well, Solomon worked on his one meal while Frenchie flitted from plate to plate to plate. Although she seemed happy to shove her face full of food, she quickly started slowing down, as if her body was unused to having so much fuel.

He waited until she was moving at a much more measured pace before speaking again. "I take it you like the diner?"

"It's all right," she deadpanned before shoving a comically huge bite into her mouth. "Passable," she said around it, the corner of her lips curling into a smirk.

"Glad you approve."

She swallowed then sat back, rubbing at her stomach. "Definitely approve. So, I'm going to need a box for all of this, and then I'll be heading out. Thanks for the charity, I guess. Maybe I'll need to tag some more megachurches if it's gonna get me all this free food."

He felt his amused mood crack a little at that. "This wasn't meant to incentivize bad behavior."

She let out a dry chuckle at that. "Oh geez, you sound like

my old Principal. Too late, consider my naughtiness incentivized."

He sighed and resisted rubbing his temples in irritation. "I don't understand why you'd rather do destructive things instead of contributing to society in a productive manner."

"Oh really?" She looked him up and down again. "And that's what you're doing? Contributing to society productively?"

"Of course." What a strange thing to ask.

She laughed again, longer and even more bitterly. "The food is nice, but you really have no idea what goes on outside of your protective little bubble, do you?"

He raised an eyebrow. "That's a pretty heavy statement to say about someone you don't know."

"But that's the thing. I know you plenty. I know, for example, that you went to really nice schools. I know that you went to some prestigious college that I could never afford. I know that you have no student loan debt or debt in general." She leaned over the table, and he found her stare had transitioned from the delightful wonder at her food to icily serious. "You've never had to worry about a utility being shut off because you didn't have enough money. You've never had to carefully calculate which bills you could be late on and which you could pay to keep things going just a little longer.

"You've never dumpster dived because you desperately needed something that you saw someone throw out. You've never had to hold the hand of a sick loved one while they begged you not to take them to the hospital because they couldn't afford it. You've never had a member of your family carted off by immigration only to be returned three weeks later without so much as a sorry.

"You know nothing outside of being rich and having everything handed to you. You don't benefit society, you feed off it like a parasite. So, I don't think you're in the proper position to comment on anything I do being destructive to society."

...what?

Solomon stared at her a moment, taken aback. It was the longest thing that she had said to him, and for once wasn't coated in thick sarcasm or wit. It was her honest, unfiltered opinion.

And apparently, her unfiltered opinion was that she hated him.

That was uncomfortable.

"I get it, you hate the rich and blame your problems on them."

"No, you clearly don't get it." She took a drink, seeming to settle into her mood. "There's nothing wrong with working hard and getting rich. That's awesome. What's wrong is exploiting other people to get that way. You need to pay livable wages, give appropriate benefits and health insurance. Treat your workers like the valuable members that they are, not just cogs in a machine. If you're not doing that, if you're nickel and diming them solely for the sake of profit, then yeah, you're a parasite. Your whole corporation is."

Solomon didn't know what to say to that. They paid their workers well above the industry standard. Where did she come off assuming things about him and his family?

But on the other hand, wasn't he actively working on changing their workers' benefits to save more money. And plenty of them had already complained about their two-thou-sand-dollar deductible—which he didn't get, two thousand dollars was hardly anything. And hadn't he just had that conversation with his brother about his housekeeper's daughter not being able to afford college?

But that wasn't his family's responsibility...right?

"You certainly have opinions," he said finally. He hadn't been prepared for a societal debate. If he was his father, he would have gotten up and dismissed everything the girl said as some sort of bleeding-heart communist.

"Yeah, why is that surprising to you? What, homeless folks can't think about anything outside of food and booze?"

There it was. The confirmation that he had been dreading. He had been struggling with trying to think of how to bring it up without sounding intrusive or insulting her if she wasn't, but she had gone and confirmed it herself.

"I never said that."

"I know, but it was implied." She looked to the waitress and waved her hand. The woman came right over, and Frenchie sweetly asked for several to-go containers. "If you don't mind, I probably should get going. I don't like wandering around after dark."

He nodded, his tongue heavy in his mouth. "At least let me drive you home. You've got a lot to carry."

And then she laughed outright at that. "Look, I loved the food, but I'm not looking to be murdered."

Yet again, he was taken aback. Not because he was hurt or took it personally, but it was something about the matter-of-factness in how she said it. Like it was a sort of threat she had to face every single day. Just part of the background tapestry of her life that wasn't worth much comment.

And that just wasn't right.

Apparently, that sent some strange signals to his brain, because he was reaching into his pocket to pull out one of his family's business cards.

"Here," he said, for all the world trying not to look like he was somehow trying to be slick. Turning it over, he scrawled out his personal cell phone number on the back before handing it to her. "Call me if you ever need anything. Things can be tough out here."

She looked down at the card then back at him, her thick eyebrow raising. "I told you, I'm not a hooker or selling myself in any way."

He knew that, and he would be lying if he wasn't getting frustrated that she thought he didn't. "Is that the only reason a person would ever want to give you their number?"

"No." She finally stopped packing up her food and gave him a serious look again. "But it's the only reason men like you would give it to a girl like me."

"A girl like you?"

She resumed her packing and stacked the food in her backpack. It was nearly full, and he found the back of his mind was weirdly prideful with the thought that she would have enough to eat for at least another day and a half.

"You know exactly what I mean," she said with finality before standing up. She gave him a curt nod. "Thanks for all the sustenance," she said before heading right out of the door, not even allowing him a chance to stand.

He looked after her until she was around the corner then pulled out his wallet to pay the bill. But as he went through the motions, he couldn't help but think about her words.

Because she'd certainly said a lot.

9

───────

Frenchie

or once, life was looking up.

Her food had managed to last her for three whole days, and that was without even trying to really scrimp. It was way easier to keep perishable stuff good during the winter, thank goodness, probably the one upside of it being increasingly cold.

And that wasn't all. It wasn't until she had settled down in her shelter, all warm and cozy in her lined hoody, when she'd reached into the pocket of her jacket and realized there was money folded up there.

Her eyes had gone wide as she'd pulled it out, realizing that the strange man had put three hundred dollars in her clothing. There was no way it hadn't been deliberate, but she'd had no idea what to do at first.

Because holy freakin' guacamole, three hundred dollars

was a *lot* of money. She remembered staring at it, wide-eyed, wondering if she was hallucinating from all the good food she had stuffed herself to bursting with.

She felt like she should probably say thank you, but she didn't have a phone to contact him, and some part of her was worried that it was some sort of bizarre, backhanded leverage to get her into a situation that she didn't want to be in. Even though he had been plenty decent at the diner, there was no telling if he was playing some sort of long con.

Once upon a time, she might have taken him for his word, but she'd long since learned not to do that.

So, she had decided to just thank him in her heart and make as much use of the money as she could.

First things first, she had bought herself a gym membership for the entire winter at a twenty-four-hour place. She could go to the sauna and shower whenever she wanted, especially if there was a particularly egregious snowstorm. Freezing to death in her sleep was suddenly much less of a threat, and it took a huge weight off her shoulders.

Then she'd bought plenty of non-perishable food and buried it in a box under her shelter. A few of the versed street veterans might spot her little hiding space, but even if she was chased out, she could probably return a couple months later and dig it back up. And if something happened to her... well, maybe they would become a lucky day for some poor soul.

Yeah, her life had practically turned around in a week, and it was pretty darn wonderful.

At the rate she was going, she was pretty sure that she could swing being hired as a seasonal worker. She had enough to buy a track phone that would work for getting the interview and then landing the job, and she could pick up two whole work outfits for maybe twenty in total at the local box store.

It was amazing how much that strange guy had changed her life, and he probably didn't even know. It was clear that three hundred dollars was absolutely nothing to him, and she wondered if he knew how many people's lives he could revolutionize so easily.

Probably not. She was aware that she didn't know him that well, but she got the feeling that he wasn't a heartless cad. He would probably want to help people if he knew how the world really was.

But she supposed that never would matter, because she was probably never going to see him again. It was clear that he had returned her hoody and had a meal with her for one of two reasons, the first being that he felt guilty for giving her the fright of her life, or he had been hoping to fulfill some fantasy about a helpless young girl but didn't have the *guts* to follow through with it.

She was leaning toward the former more than the latter, which was probably why her mind had turned back to tagging places. And why she was hanging out at one of the local spots for poor and homeless creators. It was an abandoned building by the church that she had been interrupted in the middle of tagging, but she wasn't worried about being found out.

It was just after noon, so she was alone for the most part. Most of the others were either out scrounging for food or opportunities, she assumed. And everyone would be out for rush hour, when panhandling at the side of the road had the most success. Perhaps Frenchie should have gone out there too, but she didn't want to steal from her friends when she still had a hundred dollars hidden in various parts of her clothing.

So instead she drew a dragon just for the fun of it, enjoying her music and the quiet as the back of her brain thought of where to tag next and what she wanted to say.

She was so involved with her process that she didn't notice someone coming in until whoever it was tripped over one of the old, broken chairs that dotted the room. Pulling her earbuds out, Frenchie realized it was her young friend, Tawny.

"Oh hey, did you have a good—" She cut herself off, realizing that the young woman's face was a mass of bruises, her hand pressed to her nose, which was clearly bleeding heavily. "Tawny! What happened?!?! Are you all right?"

What a stupid question. Of course, she wasn't all right. But Frenchie could see the relief on Tawny's face as she stumbled forward and collapsed into Frenchie's arms.

"Right. Stupid question. This is bad, Tawny. Real bad. I'm gonna get you some help."

Slowly she stood, hauling Tawny up with her, but when she tried to take a step, they both sank back to her knees. She was too weak.

She remembered when she was younger, how she was such a jock. She'd been strong and layered with plenty of muscle, her frame being naturally athletic. But she'd been too long on too little food and a diet that always hastily swung from stuffing as much into her face as possible to not having nearly enough.

"Hey, I'm gonna go get help, I promise, okay? Like really promise." She was loath to leave the girl alone, especially since it seemed like she couldn't even talk. "You'll be okay. I'll be gone only a minute."

Her friend nodded at her vaguely, both of her eyes so swollen that Frenchie could hardly see either of them. Gently, she set the young woman down on the floor then booked it out.

But once she was out on the street, she didn't know quite what to do. Her first instinct was to run to the nearest building and call an ambulance, but ambulances didn't like to come to their area and a lot of the EMTs treated her and her friends like junkies and prostitutes. And even if they *were* junkies and prostitutes, it still didn't really excuse the way a lot of them were treated.

Especially since they would treat Tawny like she was an idiot who got beat up by her own pimp, and that very thought made Frenchie's blood boil. Not to mention the *cost*. And there was a high chance of being turfed once she finally did make it to the ER.

No, she needed someone who would drive them to the one clinic that all of them knew that was actually kind to the ne'er-do-wells of the city. Someone who wouldn't ask questions or charge them a ridiculous amount of money.

And most importantly, someone who wouldn't try to take advantage of them with Tawny being in her weakened state.

As impossible as it was, an idea came to her instantly. For the briefest of moments, her whole body rejected it, but that quickly faded when she realized that she didn't have much of a choice.

Spotting a gas station, she bolted toward it to call Solomon.

10

Solomon

"So yeah, there will be some intense renovations, and we'll have to tear down the old silos we have, but in the end, the efficiency boost we get from this will make up for the cost within the first—"

His phone buzzed with a call and he looked to it automatically. It was rare that he ever got a telemarketer, which meant calls to his personal phone were usually either business, family, or someone he actually wanted to hear from.

So naturally, he was surprised when he saw it was an unrecognized number. Despite his better sense of judgment, he held up a finger to the twins and answered it. But never, in probably a hundred years, would he have expected to hear Frenchie on the other line, sounding terrified.

"Solomon, I need your help."

He didn't know what had made him hand his number to

her. He'd never expected her to use it. Yet at her plea, he was on in his feet in an instant.

"I have to take this," he said to the twins. "We'll catch up on this later."

"Sure, whatever you say," Silas said casually. "I have some things I need to get to as well."

Solomon nodded then rushed out, returning his attention back to the phone. "I'm on my way to the city. Where are you?"

"One second. Let me ask the gas station the address."

"Just send me your location from your phone."

She was quiet for a beat. "Solomon, I don't have a phone. I'm calling you from a landline at the gas station where I'm standing."

"Oh. Right."

He felt a bit sheepish but let that go. It wasn't weird of him to assume that she had a phone. *Everyone* had a phone. But then she was back on the line and hurriedly telling him the address, which he hastily typed into the phone while putting her on speaker.

"What's wrong? Are you hurt?"

"I... just get here, okay? I'll tell you when you're here."

"I'm about an hour out. I'll get there as soon as I can."

"All right. Thank you. And..." she seemed to hesitate, and he heard the warble in her voice as she spoke. "Please don't make me regret this."

Before he could even respond to that, the line went dead. It made sense that she probably had to rush off the phone, but he couldn't help but feel like it was another strange non-sequitur.

Shrugging it off, he dashed to his truck and drove off. It wasn't until he was nearly off their property before he realized he was rushing to the city to help a miscreant for reasons that he didn't know. He hadn't even questioned her; he'd just hopped to it.

What was going on with him?

He didn't know, and he didn't really have an answer for it, so he just kept driving.

He also might have sped a little. Or a lot. It didn't matter though, if he got pulled over; he would just pay the ticket. Whatever it was, it wouldn't be as expensive as Sal's three-hundred-dollar ticket he had managed to snag when he was just seventeen and joyriding in their father's summer convertible.

He made it to the city in record time, only slowing down once he started to be around more people. He wanted to get to Frenchie quickly, but he wasn't going to if he lost control of his truck and crashed into another innocent human. He was surprised to pass the megachurch where everything had started, but he didn't stop to think about it. In fact, he didn't stop until he saw her standing on the street, wearing the hoody that he had returned to her.

He pulled up and, to his great surprise, she went straight to his door and flopped right in. "We're going to a building around the corner. It's an old abandoned building that's boarded up. Used to be some sort of community center or church."

He nodded and did as she said, spotting the building she was talking about. It took them less than a minute to get there, and he pulled up as close as he could. Frenchie jumped out, before turning and looking back to him.

"I need you to come in."

Her particular choice of words made something jump within him, and he quickly did so, following her in.

The place was... not great. The ceiling was partially caved

in on one side, there were dips in the floor and broken boards everywhere. Strangely, there was plenty of light, but it was coming in through breaks in the wall and ceilings around them rather than any of the windows, which were completely blocked off.

And off to the left of it, there was a girl lying on the floor.

"Frenchie! Who is this? Is she all right?"

Solomon moved faster than he thought he could, and suddenly he was beside the girl. She looked even younger than Frenchie, with big, brown curls and tanned skin. That was about the only physical traits that he could pick up, however, because someone had clearly beaten the absolute snot out of her.

Frenchie said, "I need you to help me carry her out, then drive us to a clinic I know."

He looked down in absolute horror at the girl. She was dressed in even less than Frenchie was, and every visible bit of her body was covered in some sort of injury. It was awful, it was dreadful, and most of all, Solomon had a difficult time believing it was real.

And yet it was. Even as he shoved down his feelings so that he could help Frenchie carry her out, every moment confirmed just how real it was. He felt how hot her skin was the closer he was to her, burning with the effort of trying to heal herself. When his hands went under her to help haul her up, he felt how frail she was, and just how much parts of her arm were swollen.

As he and Frenchie took a couple of steps, he heard the low, pained groans from her split lips. He could smell blood on her and see tear tracks through the dirt and blood on her cheeks.

"This isn't going to work," he said, coming to a halt.

"What do you mean?"

"Let me carry her on my own. You just get the doors."

She heaved a sigh of relief as if she had expected something much worse and then nodded. Carefully, she let go of her friend, which allowed Solomon to haul her fully up in a bridal carry.

He concentrated on just walking as smoothly as he could, trying not to think about what was going on. Trying not to let the horror and rage that was rising up inside of him affect anything. Frenchie had called him because she needed him, and what she needed was for him to take care of her friend. If there was one thing Solomon was good at, it was putting his own needs aside to help others.

And the girl in his arms absolutely needed his help.

It was a much longer journey to the truck than it should have been, even though he was parked right outside. But every step made his heart jump, worried that he would cause unnecessary pain in the young woman that he was holding. When he finally got to the back door, he was aware that he was sweating much harder than he had any reason to.

"Thank you," Frenchie said breathlessly, lifting up her friend's legs and sliding into the back with her. "I mean it."

He just nodded. "Do you know the address of the clinic?"

"No, but I can give you directions."

"All right." He got into the front seat and began to drive, Frenchie calmly telling him where to turn, when finally, he thought enough to ask a question. "Shouldn't we be heading to the hospital?"

He looked back in the rearview mirror to see her shake her head. "Nah, all of the local ones will just turf us, nine times out of ten."

"Turf?" he asked. Yes, that was good. Focusing on a definition, a word. A solid fact, instead of thinking about why there was a bruised and broken girl in his back seat or who had done something so awful to her.

"Yeah, you know, when a hospital tells a patient that they're fine and to go home when they're actually sick."

Nope, that didn't make him feel any better. "Why would a hospital do that?" he asked sharply. And why was it apparently a common enough thing to have its own specific *term*?

"Because we don't have insurance. Or they're worried about drug-seeking behavior. Or they're some uppity ivy-league type that thinks being poor is a personal failure and doesn't want to treat us.

"Or because we're visibly queer, or maybe we're fat, or any reason really. There's not a lot of accountability, and they know none of us have the means to sue."

"And this happens a lot?"

"Often enough. I remember Jenny almost died because the first hospital told her she was fine, but really her common bile duct was ruptured and she had bile leaking right into her bloodstream."

"I see."

That was... a lot to digest. Hospitals were where people were supposed to go for help. It didn't make sense that they would send people away...but he also didn't think that Frenchie was lying.

So he stayed quiet because he was afraid of asking anything else that would make the situation worse. To her credit, Frenchie remained calm, just lightly stroking her friend's hair or arms and telling her that everything would be all right.

The whole situation was surreal, and that feeling didn't pass as they drove through the city. The clinic turned out to be almost a ten-minute drive, and he had no idea how Frenchie would have hauled the young woman there by herself.

Thank God that he had given her his card. Mom said that the Lord worked in mysterious ways, and he couldn't help but feel that was the case. If he hadn't... he didn't want to think about what she would have done or how long it would have taken them to get help.

He was avoiding a whole lot of thoughts, actually.

They managed to get to the clinic without any real incident, which was good because Solomon wasn't sure that he could handle much more without tumbling into a series of questions asked one right after the other.

They were greeted almost instantly by two staff members who helped get the girl onto a gurney. It was almost a bit sad that they didn't seem ruffled by it, and another came forward to ask questions of Frenchie, walking her to the back along with her friend.

And that was how Solomon ended up sitting in the small waiting room, trying to catch up with everything that had just happened. His eyes kept flitting about, going from corner to corner. He didn't understand why the clinic was so *small*. And everything looked like it came from the nineties. He didn't think that there was a single seat without a crack in it, and most of the carpet was worn thin.

His family worked with a lot of charities; why hadn't he ever heard of the name of the clinic? He was sure that they could certainly use some funding.

Ten minutes passed, maybe more, before Frenchie finally came out, her mask of calm finally cracking around her.

Solomon wasn't sure what to say, so he didn't say anything, letting her approach him. Which she did, while wringing her hands around each other. But she stopped short just in front of him, and instead began to pace.

She went back and forth once. Twice. Three times before suddenly she was talking.

"Tawny, that's my friend. Her name is Tawny. She's really talented. Plays the fiddle, dances. She does living-statue stuff around the fairs and farmer markets and busks pretty much anywhere it makes sense to. You know, with the high traffic."

All of it came out of her mouth in a rush, and he got the impression that he shouldn't interrupt. Just sit back and listen to her expel whatever she felt she needed to.

"She always does really good, but she moves around a lot. She had to have been jumped. Maybe by someone else on the circuit. Or it was just a regular mugging gone wrong? If she was dressed up as a statue, they probably knew she was carrying her tips."

What was with him and feeling like he was three miles behind the conversation? "The circuit?"

"Yeah, most of the street performers know all the good places to hit. There are some that are really adamant about always having the same places, but most work in a rotation so that they don't bore the audience. They also usually work pretty well together to make sure everyone is protected from busker-poachers."

"Busker-poachers?"

"Yeah, you know, people who specifically target and jump street performers."

Once more he was struck by the thought that something was enough of a threat to have a specific name for it, but he kept his words to himself. He was asking too many questions and perhaps stressing Frenchie out even more.

But the more seconds that passed, the more horror and

shock began to sink in. And those feelings only grew as one of the workers—was she a nurse? She was in scrubs—came back out.

"How is she?" Frenchie asked, rushing forward. "Is she okay? Is she conscious?"

"We have her on some pain medications now, and some things to prevent infection. We've helped clean up any of the wounds that she has, but she's going to need several days of rest, preferably someplace warm and not on the ground."

"Um, I don't know her living situation, but—"

"She really shouldn't be sleeping outdoors if she can manage," the nurse said.

"Okay. I think... I think I can call a shelter and see if we can get her a bed."

"If that's her only choice, then all right. But those situations can be just as dangerous. The toilets are often very far from the bed, and having that many people in a small space puts her at risk for infection. I'm sure you're already aware that the single or shared room shelters are booked up for months at a time."

Frenchie nodded and for the first time since he had met her, the girl looked lost. "I'll figure something out. When can she leave?"

"We can keep her overnight and monitor her, but we're not allowed to keep her longer than that without sending her to the hospital. We technically shouldn't be keeping her at all, but we can put down that she had a strong response to the pain medication and was deep in sleep."

"Thank you for buying us time."

"Of course. We're glad you brought her in. Spread the word to your friends that we're here and we'll do the best we can by them. The city gets more and more strict every year."

"I will. Is there anything else I can do before I head home?"

"No. Just try to be here around tomorrow at noonish to walk her home. Although she really shouldn't be walking much in her condition."

"Right. I understand. Thank you again."

"Of course. Do you need anything before you go? We haven't seen you in quite a while."

What? They knew Frenchie? That made him wonder just how, and if she had shown up at their door beaten and battered like her friend. That thought made him nauseous, and he fought to shove it back down. It wasn't his business. She was a grown woman and didn't need his protection.

"I've been having a lot better luck lately. Hopefully you won't see me for another long while after this."

"Fingers crossed. But never be afraid to come in for an exam."

"Right."

They exchanged a brief hug and then Frenchie was heading out the door.

Solomon jumped up and followed after her, unsure of what she was doing. Especially when she walked right past his truck and kept going.

"Hey, where are you off too?"

She looked back to him as if she was surprised that he was still there. "Back to the old community center. Thanks for the ride and sticking around. You're an all right guy, surprisingly."

"Thank you for calling," he said.

She nodded as if she was going to walk off, and he very much didn't want her to do that.

"I can get a hotel room," he blurted out like an idiot. Of course, the young woman stiffened and looked back at him sharply, so he blundered on. "For you and your friend. You could stay there while she recovers. It would be easier."

And safer. And warmer. But he knew better than to say those things out loud.

"But that means you have to drive out again tomorrow." She said it as if it were such a huge inconvenience.

It was just an hour's drive there, and he could do business in the city while he was at it.

He shrugged. "That's fine."

She looked like she might have wanted to refuse him for quite a while before shrugging and turning away. "All right. Where do you want us to meet you?"

"Why not here? I figure I could pick Tawny up and shuttle her to wherever is closest in case she needs follow-up care."

"You'd really do that?"

"Yeah."

"...*why?*"

He didn't know. Because the girl was in pain and deserved some comfort? Because he had the means to, so why not? Because everything that he had witnessed and learned that day was so different from his normal experiences that he wanted to see at least *some* good happen to counteract all the awful? Maybe all of them. He didn't know. But he could do something, so he wanted to.

"Why not?"

"...all right then. Noon, tomorrow, right here."

She gave another nod then turned away once more, and Solomon found himself walking quickly after her.

"Hey, what are you doing?"

"What are *you* doing?" she answered peevishly, looking out of the corner of her eye at him. Her gaze was back to being suspicious, wary, but he couldn't blame her. She'd just gotten an awful reminder of what people could do to each other.

"Trying to catch up with you. Aren't we heading to that motel?"

She stopped dead in her tracks and looked at him with the oddest expression. "...what?" Her voice was so small, so pained, it made his heart lurch in a way that he hadn't been expecting.

"I don't want to go through the hassle of hunting a place down and setting it all up when Tawny's in the car. She'll probably want to lay down and pass out as soon as she can. It just makes sense for me to get it tonight, that way you don't have to go... wherever you're staying, and you can be refreshed for taking care of her tomorrow."

Something strange shifted in Frenchie, but he didn't know her well enough to put his finger on it. All he knew was that the hairs on the back of his neck were raising, saying something about her body language, her tone, was all wrong. Her body was tense, and her eyes were shuttling back and forth as if she was trying to make a difficult decision. It felt like nearly a minute passed before she licked her lips and answered.

"...okay," was all she said, so quietly that he could hardly hear her.

"Okay," he repeated.

Another nod, and then they were walking back to his car. He unlocked it, and she slid in, her shoulders hunched, and her lips pressed thinly together. Maybe it was exhaustion hitting her. It had to be especially heady considering the adrenaline she no doubt burned through since she stumbled onto her friend.

He needed to hurry up and get her into bed before she made *herself* sick. Grabbing his phone, he started looking up if any places around the clinic would be good enough for two young women just needed somewhere safe to get well.

11

———

Solomon

$\mathcal{I}$t took more time than he would like to admit finding a place that was close enough to the clinic but not a complete roach-motel, but eventually he did. It wasn't a resort, or an any-star hotel, but it was one nice enough to have a suite with a deep tub—something he figured would be a godsend with Tawny's recovery.

He forced himself to have a cheery face, but the entire time he felt sick.

He'd always been aware that there were people who had nothing. People who struggled and went without. But he always assumed it was usually due to some sort of character flaw on their part. They didn't apply themselves or they wanted things handed to them. But Tawny and Frenchie were both so young looking. They hadn't done anything, but they faced things like being sent away from hospitals, being targeted and beaten for making money by performing. He didn't know why they didn't have jobs—he didn't even know how old they were or if they *could* work legally, but that didn't seem to matter so much anymore.

"Hey, do you need to go back and grab your things from wherever you're staying? I don't mind running out."

She stared at him sullenly before answering as if he should have known. "Everything I own is pretty much on my back."

He looked to the ratty backpack slung over one of her shoulders that was hardly full to bursting. That statement was more upsetting than it should have been, so he just continued on.

"All right, this way. I tried to get you on the first floor, but there aren't any suites there, so the second will do. At least the elevator is close by the entrance, the receptionist said."

He saw her nod in his peripheral but that was it. She seemed even more withdrawn than when he started driving, and he hoped it was just everything catching up to her. She and her friend had been through a whole lot and really, the recovery was only starting. He imagined she was going to be pretty stressed for the next week or two. At least she would be safe in the hotel.

His mind went back to that money he put in her jacket pocket. Had he unknowingly put her in danger without even thinking about it? He had no idea. But as he looked at her again, he felt like she looked a bit better—other than the expression of resigned exhaustion on her face.

Maybe he was imagining it, but her cheeks looked fuller and the dark circles under her eyes were a little less prominent. The crack in the corner of her mouth seemed to have healed, even though her lips and hands were as chapped as ever.

If that just came from having her jacket and a week of an

all right diet, he couldn't help but imagine what a week in a hotel would do for her.

The thought gave him something bright and happy to look forward to, which was a welcome change from everything that had happened since he had answered his phone. Feeling his spirit lift ever so slightly, he stepped off the elevator and headed in the direction he was pretty sure the room would be.

"The receptionist said the ice bucket is at the end of the hall, if you get thirsty. You're welcome to any of the coffee or sparkling water in the mini bar, but I ask that you don't drink the alcohol. It's always the worst tasting stuff and they charge four times the price for it."

She didn't say anything, so he just opened the door, standing to the side for her to walk in.

She did so, shoulders hunched, but he let it go. If he was in her situation, he wasn't sure he would have been able to handle it.

"So you see you have your standard bathroom, but I made sure it had a jacuzzi tub. You've got two beds over there in the bedroom, then a little kitchenette and sitting area. That way, you guys can have some fresh food if you want or maybe just heat up some pizza. I imagine you won't have much energy to cook during the next few days."

"Uh-huh."

"The receptionist said that the internet password is on the welcome card on the nightstand, and that's pretty much it. Any questions?"

Just a head shake.

He felt an odd sting of disappointment go through him. For some reason he wanted to keep talking, maybe sit on the nice couch and ask her about her life. Find out how she had ended up on the streets and what he could do to help her. But if

Frenchie was already practically non-verbal, he guessed that she probably needed time to herself to decompress and realize it was going to be all right. She wasn't alone in the situation.

"All right then, I guess—"

"Would you stop being nice and just get it over with?" she snapped, cutting him off and stopping him dead in his tracks as he went to leave.

Solomon just blinked at her a moment. He knew that he had said a few ill-advised things since they met, but he was pretty sure that he hadn't in the past few minutes. "What do you mean?"

But her hands were already pulling her shirt over her head, revealing inch by inch of her less tanned and surprisingly muscular stomach.

Solomon froze for a moment, struck by exactly what was happening. It felt like he was moving through molasses and she was going at the speed of light, whipping her garment all the way off and throwing it to the side.

She wore an old sports bra, one that was more gray than white. He knew he shouldn't be looking, but he felt like he was in a sort of shock. One moment he had been talking, the next she was getting naked in front of him.

But then her hands went to the button of her jean shorts and he jolted back to reality. Gripping one of them, he held it still.

"Stop," he rasped, trying to keep his eyes on the ceiling, on her face, anything but the valley of her cleavage below, or the stories that her bare skin showed. Even with him trying his best, he saw a long scar over one shoulder, and one looked like a birthmark on her side. Three small, circular marks sat just below her collarbone, almost silvery-white against her tanned skin.

Thankfully, however, she did. Freezing just as he had been just moments earlier. She was stiff, but she allowed him to gently push her hands to her side and step away.

"What are you doing?" he asked finally, his tongue once again feeling heavy in his mouth. He swore that the girl was running by rules that he didn't understand, that he didn't even know, and his head was beginning to hurt from it.

Her voice was barely a whisper when she spoke. "I... the hotel room... You bought it tonight because..." She licked her lips, and finally, she looked up at him. It was in that stare that he realized just how young and small she was and the position of power he had over her. "I thought you wanted me to... repay you? For my friend?"

And then all of it hit him at once.

Oh goodness. Oh goodness no! It took all of his control to keep his world from shattering around him and flipping out. She didn't think he was *helping* her. She didn't think he was providing her shelter because she needed it and he could. She thought he was *buying* her.

Her friend's life for her own body. How many times had she told him that she wasn't selling herself? But when it came down to procuring what her friend needed, she was willing to make that sacrifice—a sacrifice that she had in no way been willing to make before.

No.

No, no, *no!*

He needed to move, needed to do *something,* so he walked to where she had thrown her shirt then handed it to her carefully.

"Frenchie, that's not what's happening here." He was sick again. Because he was beginning to realize that the reason the young woman was so sure that he was going to take advantage of her was because so many people must have tried before. And maybe they succeeded.

No, he couldn't think of that at all, because then he really would lose his lunch and he had a feeling that was the last thing Frenchie needed to see.

"You never have to do anything like that with me. Or anybody for that matter. Like you said, you're not for sale."

With that he retreated all the way to the door, ready to make a break for it. He vaguely recognized if this were any other situation, that his body might have been excited by seeing such a beautiful woman so bare in front of him, but he couldn't get past the horror of the situation. The implication of it all.

But Frenchie didn't look any less relieved. "But… that doesn't make any sense. Why else would you buy me a hotel room? Why else would you get all of this for us?"

"Because you needed it."

"People don't do things like this. They don't go out and drop money on people for nothing. Even charities are a write-off."

He didn't have an answer for her, so instead he just opened the door and stepped outside. "Goodnight, Frenchie, please try to rest. You have the only key card, so I'll meet you at the clinic tomorrow."

And then he closed the door because he really didn't think that he could handle anything else.

He managed to keep himself in check all the way until he got into his truck, but then his hands went to the top of his head and he let out a cry of frustration. As soon as he got home, he was definitely going to have to hit up his personal gym so that he could vent some of the frustration that was building up so intensely in him. He felt like if one more thing happened that he just might pop then and there.

He was a king of suppression, of always maintaining his composure, but the day's events had seriously challenged him. When he was done yelling, he put the keys in the ignition and drove home. But the entire way there, he had to force himself not to think about who Frenchie had known in the past to make her think all the things that she did.

That was one road he knew he shouldn't go down.

12

———

Frenchie

She stared at the door, eyes wide, heart pounding, and understanding absolutely *nothing*.

A rich man was buying her things, helping her, setting her up in a *really* fancy hotel room, but he didn't want... *her?*

That didn't compute. It made absolutely no sense and went against everything she knew. Rich people didn't help others for nothing. Everything was money, profit, and transactions to them. Everything was about gain, gain, gain, so he had to want *something* from her.

And yet he was gone, and she was the one in the room, the room key laying on the table to her right.

Rushing to the door, she slid the chain into the lock before sliding the additional deadbolt for protection. She stepped back a moment, then thought better and got a chair to put under the handle.

There.

That made her feel slightly better.

Feeling like she was in a daze, she walked over to the bedroom area. She couldn't believe how big the room was. When he said that he was going to get them a hotel, she'd been shocked. She'd fully been about to tell him exactly where to shove it when she realized that having a safe place indoors for the week was going to be Tawny's best bet at recovery. Frenchie had seen what a bad infection could do to someone like them. It had been old Mike who'd gotten a cut in his foot, and by the time he got enough money up to go get it treated, the infection had moved to his blood and he'd gone septic. He never left the hospital after that, and since none of Frenchie or her friends were kin, the hospital wouldn't release his ashes to them either.

She didn't want that for Tawny, so she'd agreed, even knowing what it was going to cost her.

...except it didn't seem to be costing her anything?

She flung herself back on the bed, so exhausted she could cry. Except she hadn't cried since she was eighteen and had no intention of starting that back up again.

Not that she had been much of a crier before that. Her stepfather had assured that much. He always said that she had been manipulating him with her tears, that she was trying to trick him, so he'd taken to putting out his cigarettes on her or making her stick her hands in hot water until she stopped.

Her fingers idly went up to the three small circles just above her collarbone, tracing them as she recalled the look of shock on the rich cowboy's face as she'd been shirtless in front of him. His expression had been so alarmed that it had actually managed to make her forget how upset she was for just a moment. ...was she reading everything wrong?

Sleep rushed up on her fast despite how worried she was about everything. When was the last time she had slept in a real bed? It had to at least been a summer earlier. She'd been on the road with a traveling carnival and a flash flood had forced all of them to be housed in a hotel for the night. And even then, it'd been three to a bed for all the non-performers and management. The last time she'd had such a large bed entirely to herself was *years* ago.

Kicking off her shoes, she thought back to the moment when she'd been standing in front of Solomon, his large hands on her wrists. How had she never noticed just how big his hands were before? He could have easily broken her arm, or overtaken her, but he looked more horrified than anything else. Like the idea of him being able to buy her was truly awful.

And it was, but she wasn't used to *other* people thinking that.

He'd looked so alarmed in that moment that it had startled her too, leaving the two of them staring at each other like a couple of morons.

What a wild ride.

Scooting up the blanket, she fully meant to tuck herself under the covers. But all she managed was to grab a pillow and put it under her head before she was slipping right into her slumber.

FRENCHIE PACED OUTSIDE of the clinic, wondering for the twentieth time or so if she had died and her entire experience over the past few days was just some sort of very in-depth illusion. Because really, any sort of "life flashing before her eyes" thing would be far too depressing.

When she had woken up, she'd been startled more than anything, unable to figure out where she was or why her back and shoulders didn't ache. But then things came rushing back to her and she felt her cheeks color.

Oh, goodness gracious, she really had taken her shirt off right in front of Solomon and basically accused him of soliciting her for prostitution! She was such an *idiot!* But what else was she supposed to think? He'd obviously dropped some serious *bank* on her and she had no idea what to think of that.

She still didn't, as she paced, but she had decided to stop obsessing over it and just sort of deal with things as they happened. She'd always been pretty good at thinking on her feet, and as long as Tawny was safe, she was pretty sure that she could get them out of any bad situation, no matter how sticky.

Besides, even if everything all went to crap, she sure did enjoy the steaming hot shower she had taken in the morning, standing there for about half an hour or so while she scrubbed all of the grossness off of her.

It had been weird, not having to rush out to get herself warm or to beat the crowds at the gym to use a shower, or to grab stale bagels. Instead, she puttered around, stretched, then went to the hotel laundry and paid a couple dollars of quarters to wash all her clothes that she wasn't wearing. Which wasn't a lot, but hey, it was exciting to have something freshly laundered.

She had finished everything up that she could to occupy herself, it was still only ten. But she figured that she could get to the clinic early and make sure that Tawny had the go-ahead to leave. Besides, it felt strange not to walk at all, and she figured the fresh air would do her some good.

She'd arrived without anything exciting happening, but

when she'd gone in, the nurse had said that Tawny was still sleeping it off so they didn't want to wake her right away. Which meant instead of visiting with her friend and catching her up on everything that had happened, she was stuck just waiting around.

And Frenchie had never been very good at waiting. Hence, the pacing.

But unlike usual, it wasn't doing anything to calm her, and she only felt relief when she saw Solomon's familiar fancy truck pull up.

He still mystified her, and his bizarre actions made her stomach twist with dread and anticipation, but she would be lying if she also didn't feel a strange sort of happiness at seeing him again. Although his questions could be annoying and he really had *no* idea how the world worked, he was strangely good at dealing with things. He hadn't freaked out like she thought he would when he'd first seen Tawny. He'd been calm and collected, in fact. He didn't demand to know what happened to her, or why someone had smacked her around so hard; he'd just done whatever Frenchie said she needed.

She wrinkled her nose as her mind connected those dots. Considering his actions, maybe she could afford to give him the benefit of the doubt.

But that was hard for her. The last non-homeless person she had really trusted had led to her almost being carted all the way back home. It was only her flexibility and some quick thinking that had gotten her out of that, and she didn't really need a repeat experience.

"And here I thought I was early," Solomon said as he got out of his car. A cup of to-go coffee in both of his large hands.

He was dressed more casually than she had seen him before, in a soft-looking T-shirt and black sweatpants. She wasn't sure if he was aware of how the fabric of his top clung slightly to his muscles, showing just how built he was, but she certainly didn't think she could bring it up without sounding creepy.

"You are. I'm just earlier."

It took a lot of her willpower not to let out a huge sigh of relief that he wasn't being weird about what had happened the night before. She had almost been afraid that he wouldn't show at all, leaving her alone to get Tawny to the hotel he had bought for them, but she guessed her worry was for nothing.

"Here, I got you this," he said, handing her the coffee. "Like you had it in the diner, two sugars, one cream."

She found herself staring at him in surprise. Not only had he paid attention to how she had ordered her coffee, but he'd *remembered* it? She was beginning to wonder if he was some sort of handsome alien rather than a human being. That certainly made more sense than all of his bizarre giving-spree, considering they had met when he'd chased her down for daring to tag his family's property.

"Thanks," she barely remembered to say, her hand shaking a little as she took the cup. It was still piping warm in her hands, and she hugged it to herself gratefully. She was aware that she'd been a bit... rude a couple of times to the man, but it was because she had been so certain of his intentions. After all, the world played by a very specific set of rules, and she had learned most of them the hard way.

But what if... what if she was wrong?

No. That wasn't possible.

"I hope you don't mind, but I grabbed a couple of things I thought the two of you might need so you can bum around in the hotel and not have to do anything."

She didn't miss the flush that instantly colored his high

cheekbones. Goodness, he really had some bone structure, didn't he?

He grimaced then said, "Sorry, I shouldn't have said bum. I—"

Of all the things for him to be worried about! She couldn't help it; she let out a soft laugh and just shook her head. "It's fine. I understood what you meant. You're a bit jumpy, aren't you?"

He stood a respectful distance away from her, and she wondered if it was because of her stupid move the night before.

"Must be the caffeine," he deferred smoothly. "Why are we outside?"

"Tawny's still passed out. Apparently, she either is really sensitive to the drugs or she was pulling too many all-nighters in a row. Which, thinking about it, she probably was if she was traveling."

"She couldn't sleep on the bus or train?"

"She's a seventeen-year-old girl traveling on her own. She can't sleep anywhere in public without risk."

"Right. Of course."

An interesting thing happened. It was something she had only barely noticed the day before, but with a full night's sleep, she found herself alert enough to catch it in real time. Occasionally, when she said a particularly grim thing about life, Solomon would go a little gray, the corners of his mouth turning downward. It wasn't a full-on frown, like he was disagreeing with her or thought she was lying, but he definitely seemed affected by what he was learning.

Which was interesting all on its own.

"Have you eaten yet today?"

She started, having slipped into her own head for a minute. "Oh, no. I haven't. Nerves, I guess."

"I see a street vendor a little way down the road, want to walk? I could go for a taco or gyro."

She squinted her eyes in the direction he pointed and thought she maybe saw the glint of a silver cart. Suddenly, her stomach gave a rumble and she found herself licking her lips once again. She really needed to stop doing that; they were already so chapped.

"Sure, I could go for some food."

"All right."

And then he was walking off, leaving Frenchie to hurry after him.

Geez, he had some long legs. It took her two and a half steps for every one of his, and if she wasn't already a quick walker, she would have been left in the dust. She took in his height and muscles and the confident way he walked.

Not bad.

He glanced over his shoulder—no doubt to check if she was still following, and she tore her gaze away from his body and tried to look just past him. She wasn't sure how successful she was at that.

It definitely seemed that she was rusty when it came to checking someone out. Then again, she couldn't remember the last time that she had been attracted to someone who wasn't on a movie screen. Her world didn't have romance, and it wasn't like she trusted anyone enough for that anyway.

But when she looked at Solomon's broad shoulders, and his handsome face with those eyes that always seemed to be asking so much, she couldn't help but feel the tiniest sliver of... of... well it was *something*, even if it was so small that she could barely feel it flickering alongside the fear and apprehension.

They made it to the food cart within a few minutes and without any more of him catching her staring awkwardly at things she shouldn't be looking at. He ended up ordering a couple of tacos for himself while Frenchie got kebabs. She figured she might as well stock up on protein while the going was good.

Solomon still kept a respectful distance from her as they waited for their food, his gaze either up in the sky or solidly on her face. She couldn't help but feel a bit of embarrassment in the back of her mind as they stood there. Was he thinking about what she looked like without her shirt? She knew her bra was old, and she wasn't generously endowed like a pinup girl, or flared out with wide hips like the models du jour, but she didn't think she was that bad either.

Was he repulsed by her, or was he just trying to be a good Christian boy? She didn't know, and she couldn't think of a way to find out either. So many Christians that she met weren't very Christlike at all, and it was impossible to tell them apart from the real deal.

"These are good," he said in surprise as they headed back to the clinic.

Frenchie noticed that his pace had changed, going at about half the speed he had before. That was a relief because she wasn't sure about what technique would be best when it came to speed-walking while eating meat off a pointy stick.

"Yeah, we really have the best food trucks around here. NYC folks always brag, but they don't really compare."

"You've been to New York?" he asked casually. Or at least he tried to ask casually. But she could see in the corner of her eye how his shoulders straightened, and his posture became more attentive. He was curious, but he wanted to respect her privacy, it seemed. How utterly novel.

"I've been almost everywhere but Alaska and Hawaii."

"You travel a lot?"

"I used to. I've been sticking around the west for the most part over the past three years."

"Did something change?"

She shrugged, feeling like she had divulged enough. "Life's always changing, isn't it?"

"I suppose." He didn't say anything further, seeming to understand that she was done. For someone who had been raised with a silver spoon, he seemed surprisingly empathetic. Or maybe she was just being a bit enamored because he'd helped her so much. He was no longer the scary boogeyman who had chased her down twice and scared the absolute pants off her. Instead, he was the confusing and backward rich guy who she couldn't puzzle out.

She'd always been good at puzzles.

They didn't talk a lot on the way back, just eating and chewing. And yet it was nice.

Frenchie hadn't quite realized just how much winter isolated a lot of the people in her situation. They didn't tag as much because it was harder to work with the spray-paint when it felt like their fingers were going to fall off from the cold, and even harder to keep the paint from being ruined. Not to mention that everyone was so set on trying to find shelter, stay warm, and get food that their usual hangouts and meeting places sort of fell by the wayside.

It was nice to just be next to someone, sharing a human activity. Even if she didn't entirely trust the handsome man. But she also didn't... not trust him.

They made it back to the clinic with only a half-hour passing, and that was with them seriously slowing down on their return walk. Frenchie finished the last of her kebab and downed her coffee, throwing it in the trashcan outside of the clinic.

"You really don't have to do this, you know."

He shrugged again, and she wasn't sure what to make of it. "I want to."

"So you've said." She studied his face, trying to figure him out. Every time she felt like she had him pegged, he would go and do or say something ridiculous. Sometimes, she felt like they were speaking different languages. "But why do you want to? Did you like... murder someone and you're trying to make up for it? Did a ghost of Christmas Past come and tell you that you need to change your ways?"

"No, nothing like that," he answered with an easy smile, and if that didn't make her heart skip a beat. What was that about? "And FYI, it would have been Jacob Marley, if we're going by the classics."

"Eh, I never read it. I always just preferred to watch the Muppets' version every time it came on. The Marley brothers had the best song," Frenchie said.

"I... don't think I've ever watched that."

She couldn't help it when she turned to him with wide eyes. "You've never seen *A Muppet's Christmas Carol*!?"

"Why do you say that like it's a crime against humanity?"

"Because it practically is! *A Muppet's Christmas Carol* has the best songs, the best costuming, and some of the best puppetry of all the specials that start playing around the holidays."

"Uh-huh, and you are a completely unbiased expert," he said, his eyebrows raising.

"I'll have you know that I am. I'm certified, one hundred percent holiday movie special extraordinaire."

"Ah, forgive me for ever doubting your knowledge then. I should have known better." He chuckled.

"Yeah, you definitely should have. And who knows, maybe I'll forgive you if you show that you understand the error of your ways."

"And just how am I supposed to do that?"

She found herself smiling as she answered. It was like being back in the diner, except she was about five times more relaxed than she was that day.

"By watching the movie, of course."

"Right, right. The answer is so obvious now."

She looked up at him, worried that she was pushing it too far, but she saw that easy smile was on his face and for once, he didn't look worried or confounded. It was a good look for him, and she couldn't help but wonder if she was a normal girl, and he was a normal guy, if there could ever be something between them.

Wait, no, why was she thinking like that? She needed to shove that thought out of her head immediately.

Her mind scrambled for something to distract her, so the next thing she knew, her mouth was blurting something out.

"So how old are you if *A Muppet's Christmas Carol* wasn't a part of your childhood?"

He hesitated for a moment, his eyebrows going up to his thick hairline. He couldn't be older than his forties, but then again, with rich people it was so difficult to say.

"I'm thirty-two. Going to be thirty-three in a few months," he answered.

"Huh, so you're like a decade older than me. That's wild."

"You're twenty-three?"

"Yup and have been for about four months. So really, you're nine and a half years, but a decade sounds better."

"Oh yes," he said flatly. "That sounds *so* much better."

"Aw, come on, don't be salty just because you're old."

"I'm not *old*," he huffed. "And what on earth does salty mean?"

That surprised her. "You have to be kidding me. Everyone knows what salty means."

"I guess that everyone doesn't, because I don't have any idea." He squinted at her, rubbing his strong jaw. "I reckon you're not gonna tell me, are you?"

"Nope. I'm sure your ancient brain just wouldn't be able to handle it."

If he were anyone else, she might have been worried about setting him off. Her mouth had gotten her into trouble ever since she could remember, and there was only so much teasing people could take before they eventually lashed out. But Solomon just huffed another laugh and crossed his arms.

"I'm beginning to feel very attacked here."

"Oh, *are* you? That's a shame. Truly a shame."

"Really? Because your tone says otherwise."

She couldn't help it, she cackled outright. When was the last time she had laughed like this? She didn't know, but she enjoyed the sensation.

"Hey, what time is it?" he asked.

Frenchie looked at him blankly, holding up her hands in a "how should I know" gesture.

"I don't have a phone, dude. But my internal clock is pretty good, so if I had to guess, we're somewhere between twelve fifteen and twelve thirty."

He squinted his eyes suspiciously and pulled his own phone from his pocket. Geez, it really was huge! Bigger than his hand, and that was saying something. He pressed a button on the side then gave an appreciative nod.

"Twelve twenty-five. Not bad."

"You get a good sense of it when you're wandering around."

"I bet. I never even think about it, you know. If I need to check the time, I am always close to something that can tell me."

"Ah, a luxury." She closed her eyes, remembering all the times when she used to have something to carry around. "But also, sometimes it's really freeing not living your whole life by a time clock."

"And that's what I'm doing?"

She shrugged, peaking at him with one of her eyes. "Is it not? I don't know your life, I'm just assuming."

He didn't answer, and she watched his face carefully to see if he was angry, but he just seemed contemplative. Huh, that wasn't the first time that he didn't answer because he seemed to be *really* thinking about her words, and she didn't know what to do with that. She was used to people brushing her off or dismissing her if she said something controversial, strange, or decidedly "Frenchie." But he didn't do that. How bizarre.

"Well, do you think we should go in and check to see if she's up? It's been about an hour and a half almost since I got here."

"Yeah, that sounds like a good idea," Frenchie said.

They walked inside, him holding the door for her, and the receptionist nodded to her from the desk.

"She's up now," the woman said quickly, but not impolitely. "But she's still coming around, and they're going over all the care she needs to do to make sure she doesn't get an infection or reinjure herself. You're probably looking at another half hour or so."

"That's fine," Frenchie said automatically, more relief flooding through her. She had been worried that something would go wrong. "We can wait."

"Actually, I'll have you fill out these papers for her. I figure you know the drill."

"Yeah, I do."

Frenchie took the clipboard and went to sit down, Solomon following her. When she sat, she couldn't help but notice that he sat a seat away from her. Weird.

"What did she mean by that?" he asked.

"These outtake forms require a lot of info we don't have, like current address and things like that. We all have some bullhonkey answers we write down with local shelters we're on good terms with, or the number of one of the good social workers around. You know, the usual."

"Nothing that you ever say sounds usual," he muttered under his breath, which made her chuckle.

"I told you, you live in a bubble. All this stuff is just the real world for us poor folks."

He made a noncommittal sound and she returned her attention back to the paperwork. She didn't want to make Tawny wait a second longer than she had to.

The minutes ticked by and she did indeed end up handing the clipboard back before Tawny came out. In the back of her mind, she tried not to think of how much time Solomon was spending on her, from driving an hour one way to driving an hour back and how much he was sitting around. Considering how much he made, his time had to be costly, and yet he didn't even look agitated as he waited for Tawny to be released.

When she finally was, they took their time getting her to the truck, setting her up against some pillows in the back seat so that she could prop her legs up. Apparently, she'd twisted her knee pretty badly, resulting in it being dislocated, and they'd popped it back into place at the clinic. Frenchie was grateful she hadn't been around for that part. She'd dislocated her shoulder twice when she was younger, and it wasn't something that she would want a repeat of.

"Where are we going?" Tawny said once they were driving along. Her voice was much raspier than usual, and Frenchie tried not to think of why.

"My friend Solomon here set us up with a room for your recovery."

Frenchie didn't miss the look Tawny gave her through the rearview mirror. She just shrugged in response, her shoulders coming up to her ears. Thankfully, the young girl seemed to understand. And if she had any questions about how or why that had happened, she didn't ask. Tawny was good that way. She really just wanted to make her money and save up enough to get to California, where she was hoping to join a dance troupe. Frenchie's heart dropped when she wondered just how much the girl had been set back by the attack. Hopefully she had been burying and hiding her money too; otherwise, whoever had attacked her had made off with thousands. Frenchie didn't know her exact finances, but she knew that Tawny needed at least four grand to get there and have a place to stay, and she'd been working hard since she was fifteen.

Ugh, it was all so depressing. It seemed like any time one of them took a few steps forward, something would push them a million steps back. It was exhausting.

As if to punctuate her point, Tawny fell asleep on the short drive to the hotel. It was less than ten minutes, but she was out like a light. They parked, and Frenchie didn't want to move her right away.

Solomon said, "Why don't you wait here with her while I take the stuff I bought up to the room? I don't think we should leave her alone, but I don't think we should wake her up just yet."

"Yeah, that's fine."

"All right, I'll make sure to take my time."

He got out, making sure to shut the door quietly after he pressed a button that she guessed popped the trunk. It wasn't until he fully disappeared around the back of the truck that she realized he left his keys in the ignition.

Wow, that was a pretty huge sign of trust. Especially considering that he was going inside to the building on the second floor. It would be so easy to drive off with it and take it somewhere that could strip it before they ever got caught. His truck was really high end, she had no doubt that she could get enough to set her up for months. Maybe even turn her life around completely.

Except she would never do that. Period. And especially never do that to someone that had helped both her and her friend. Her stepfather may have had some choice words about her, but when it came down to it, she did have morals and principals, and stealing someone's truck didn't fit into the paradigm.

Closing her eyes, she let herself sit back against the seat for a moment. Her belly was full, her feet didn't hurt, and her friend was safe with her again. For how awful the day before had been, things were certainly looking up. She had to be careful not to get too used to it, because it was all going to end after a week.

But still, a whole lot could be done in a week. Especially if —after the first day of making sure Tawny was all right on her own—Frenchie went down to the reception area and used one of the lobby computers. She could go grab that track phone she had been thinking about and fill out some online applications, really take advantage of all the time she had been given.

She was so deep into her mental plans that she nearly jumped when a knock sounded on her door. It was Solomon, and since his keys were inside the truck, he was locked out.

Rolling down the window, she batted her eyes at him. "Can I help you, sir?" she teased.

He cracked a smile at that. "You ready to get out? It's been about fifteen minutes or so, but we can just sit for a while, if you like."

Frenchie looked at Tawny, who was passed out so hard that she was drooling a bit on one of the pillows he had piled in the back.

"We can talk."

He smiled at that and went around the truck, sliding into the driver's seat. Frenchie was already set with a question for him as soon as he settled in.

"You're a part of the Miller family, right?"

He grimaced, and she wondered why. "You looked us up?"

"No. I don't really have steady access to the internet. But when you mentioned I tagged several of your family's places, I guessed you had to be a part of that rich Christian ranch family I hear on the news every so often."

"You listen to the news?"

"I overhear things, mostly. Funny, you don't really seem like much of a cowboy."

"I don't?"

"Sure, this is what... the fourth, fifth time we've met and you haven't yee-hawed even once."

He laughed, shaking his head at her. "Ah yes, because that is the measure of whether or not someone is a true cowboy."

"That's what John Wayne taught me. What, are you telling me you have a trusty steed that's always by your side and a loyal dog?"

His mirth faded a bit, and his stare out of the window grew heavy. "I don't. For being the heir of our ranching operation, I don't actually spend much time on the ranch."

"Well that's a real shame," she said. "If I had a ranch, I would be petting all the animals every single day."

"Oh really? You like animals."

"I *love* animals. I miss having a pet, but I really travel around too much. Although I was thinking about maybe befriending a stray dog for protection's sake, but that means all my stray cat friends will stop hanging around."

"Our ranching operation is huge. It would take me days to pet every animal, let alone play with them."

"So?"

He gave her a reproachful look. "What do you mean, so?"

"You're rich! So what if it takes you two days to pet all of them. Just spend the two days petting them then. What's the point of having a mega-corporation if you can't enjoy the good things in life?"

"And the good things in life are petting all the livestock in my family's business?"

She reached over and playfully swatted his arm. "The good things in life are being able to boop snoots and pet the heads of all the wonderful creatures on your property."

"That's one way to look at it."

"Come on, you're telling me the heir of the Miller fortune doesn't even make time to ride his horse?"

"It's been... a couple weeks."

His tone said it was more than that. Interesting.

"Huh, I can't imagine being as loaded as you and not using it to actually enjoy yourself."

He didn't say anything to that, and the conversation petered out. She didn't mind, however, thinking of what it would be like to walk out of her house and be able to saunter over to a beautiful horse, or even *horses.*

She'd been able to see plenty of the noble creatures in her travels, and even ridden one a couple of times at the carnivals and shows she got gigs at. It was something she never got tired of, and maybe if it wasn't so cold, she'd walk as far as she could out of the city until she reached ranch country where she could draw them to her heart's content.

The quiet lasted on for a while before Solomon shifted. "Do you think we've given her enough time?"

Frenchie looked back to Tawny, who had stopped drooling, her chin was resting solidly on her chest.

"Yeah, let's get her into a bed. It'll probably be the softest thing she's slept on in months."

They both got out of the truck and went about the slow process of waking her up and helping Tawny out of the truck and inside. The receptionist didn't say anything about the sorry state of the young woman between them, and Frenchie was eternally grateful for that.

They reached the door and Solomon helped her walk to one of the beds, where Tawny immediately fell right back asleep. Well, it was good for her to know that she had an opioid sensitivity while she was young.

"And she didn't have anything to carry up, right?" Solomon asked, turning to Frenchie. She just shook her head, trying not to think about Tawny's beloved fiddle and one of her tools that helped her earn as much money as she did.

She wasn't sure if someone had stolen her fiddle, or if she had been so beaten that she couldn't carry it with her...

Ugh, best not to think about such things.

"All right, well, I tried to get everything I could think of that you guys might use, but call me again if I forgot something important."

"Huh?" She followed his gesture to the table in the room, where she saw several bags were stacked. Wait... *what?*

Wide-eyed, she walked over and opened one. There was lotion inside, toothbrushes, toothpaste, and mouthwash. Shampoo and conditioner of several types, soap, and deodorant. The next bag even had feminine products in it. It looked as though he had gone into the store and gotten one of everything.

The next bag had food, cereal bars and toaster pastries, bagels and bread. There were also some regular protein bars and pretzels. The bag after that had microwave pizzas, frozen fruit, and some desserts as well. Beef pockets in another along with microwave burritos, sour cream, salsa, and cheese. It was enough to fill the fridge and freezer in the kitchenette and maybe one of the cabinets too.

And yet *another* bag had rubbing alcohol, witch hazel, cotton swabs, and everything else that Tawny might need to heal. Also socks, several pairs of leggings, and about a dozen or so of those multi-underwear packs in different sizes.

It was all so *much.*

Once again, she was struck by the peculiarity of it all. Was he... was he gay? Was he playing some sort of strange long con? Nothing made sense!

"Did I miss something?" he asked cautiously, as if he was so sure that he had done something wrong. "Is there something else I should have done for y'all?"

"No," she managed to say without her voice warbling. "You've done more than we could ever ask for. Really."

He nodded, seemingly surprised by her answer. And that

seemed to be a good enough answer for him because he headed toward the door.

"It doesn't feel that way," he mumbled.

"What was that?"

But then he was already out, the door shutting behind him, leaving Frenchie to stare after him.

Huh. Well that was something.

Glancing to Tawny to make sure she was settled, Frenchie gave herself a moment to breathe. And once she was done with that moment, she went back to the table and started to put things away.

13

Solomon

"Hey there, pretty lady. It's been a while, hasn't it?"

Maribella whinnied at him, shaking her head playfully before letting him pet along her muzzle. Her gray fur was as soft as ever, her muscles jumping under his fingertips before his hand went to her mane.

"Would you like a braid in your hair? You've always been a bit vain, haven't you?"

She wuffled at him, her mouth searching his pockets for treats. He pulled one out for her before he started on a section of her mane, twisting strands around like his cousin, Benji, had taught him.

Dad had said it was a useless skill, back when the teenaged Benji had shown Sam, Solomon, and Silas how to do it, but Solomon had liked learning it. Sure, it wasn't particularly profitable, and he didn't get to do it often, but it was a nice thing to do every once in a while.

Something about Frenchie's words in the truck had stuck with him. When *was* the last time that he had actually enjoyed the liberties that living on a ranch afforded him? He couldn't remember. He was so caught up in the business side of things that he had forgotten about the parts that he loved so much.

"Would you like to go for a ride along with Caspian?" Little Maribella was too small for his stature, having been meant for Mom after her primary mount was retired, but then Mom had developed arthritis in her hips and lower part of her spine and given up riding altogether. As a result, poor Maribella didn't get out much.

Actually, none of their horses did lately.

The beautiful gray girl nodded enthusiastically as if she understood, but she probably just recognized the lead in his hands. Laughing, he went through the motions of tethering her to Caspian's saddle then headed out of the barn.

For being cooped up for so long, she sure did wait politely for him to mount up once they were outside, dancing in place slightly. But once he started at an even trot, her excitement rang out in a happy whinny.

"That's my girl," Solomon said, feeling a warmth in his chest that he hadn't in a while. "I'll make sure you get out more often, but for right now, how about a walk around as much of the perimeter as we can get?"

She let out another agreeable sound that he interpreted as her saying yes and picked up the pace ever so slightly. Their ranching operation was far too large to go around in any sort of reasonable time, but maybe he was in the mood to be a little unreasonable.

The cool, crisp air reminded him of when he was much younger... when his cousins would come visit and they would set up a couple of tents out in the fields and tell creepy stories around the campfire.

And also girls, but Bart was really the only one who had much to say about that. Benedict had a girlfriend pretty much as long as Solomon could remember, but he was always pretty tight-lipped about the whole thing.

He could almost taste the smores and woodsmoke on the back of his tongue, a hint of memories he hadn't thought about in ages.

What had happened to all of that?

He knew as the years passed that Dad and Uncle Douglas had sort of fallen out. Uncle Douglas was a man of very few words, but strong convictions, and apparently, he felt like his younger brother was too obsessed with profit and gain over everything else. Something about not treating the animals nicely enough and becoming obsessed with wealth. But Solomon didn't understand that considering that Uncle Douglas and Aunt Annie Miller were incredibly well off too. Not billionaires—well, except for Bryant—but they weren't going to be poor anytime soon. In fact, they could sell everything the next day, never work again, and their grandchildren would still probably be just as comfortable.

Yet somewhere along the way, Solomon couldn't help but feel like his family *had* lost touch. But why hadn't he noticed it until recently?

He rode past the silos that contained the feed for the animals—sorghum, milo, and grains. They had acres and acres of fields for that, rotating them in cycles to let the earth rest. Then he passed by the birthing pens for when it was breeding time for the steers. The McLintoc Miller Ranch was *not* a dairy ranch, but they had a partnership with several of the other dairy farms in the area so that any females born went to them, and the males stayed with Solomon's family for finishing. Then there were the rice and wheat crops. The corn. The cotton. The peanuts and the sugar cane.

It didn't seem like much, and yet it was their whole lives. They'd dropped their sheep, dropped their goats, and it seemed like the workers spent more time with their horses than his own family ever did. They were so disconnected to the earth under their feet. They'd forgotten what it was like to watch the sun come up, the morning dew coating the grass before sizzling off in the heat.

And that made him feel... empty?

He found himself swinging between happy and content while riding along and wondering what had happened. Was he blowing everything out of proportion? Was he letting some homeless girl from the city get into his head?

Because he was thinking about her an awful lot. Even his dreams wouldn't let him rest from her, playing out dozens of different ways. Sometimes it was her that he had found beaten on the floor, face covered in blood and swollen. Sometimes it was that he was chasing her but he never got any closer. Sometimes it was her screaming at him, telling him that she hated him and he was a total creep.

But sometimes, when he was deeply asleep, they were what could have happened if he hadn't stopped her from removing her clothes. But those were always the worst, really, because those dreams made him out to be everything that she was afraid of. And even if some part of him enjoyed what happened, enjoyed picturing what it would feel like to have her lips pressed against his, her *body* against his, he felt so intensely guilty because he knew it wasn't what she wanted. What if he really was just like she thought, and he was just better at hiding it? And all the cold showers in the world didn't help him feel less scuzzy.

Was he helping her just because he was drawn to her? She seemed insistent on the idea that no one did anything for free, so what if she was right? Did he have some subconscious reason for doing all that he'd done? ...or did he just want to protect her because she was a human and deserved to feel safe?

Even after a solid week of thinking, he didn't have an answer, and he certainly didn't have one when his phone rang.

He recognized the hotel number instantly and answered. He wasn't sure what he expected. This was the last day at the hotel—at least that he'd paid for—so he'd been hoping they would touch base before disappearing entirely.

"Hey, Frenchie, everything all right?"

"How did you know it was me?"

"I called my phone from your hotel room when I was there and saved it under your name so I'd know it was you if you called."

There was a strange pause there for a moment. "Wow, you really think of everything, don't you?"

"Well, I don't know about that, but I certainly try."

There was her little laugh. He had missed it, but he knew he absolutely shouldn't have. Frenchie was a whole decade younger than him and *homeless.* She was what his father would call a bleeding-heart hippie, but then again, Dad called almost everyone a bleeding-heart hippie.

"Yeah, I'm starting to get that. Anyway, Tawny and I went to the clinic today. They said she won't need another checkup for a month as long as she doesn't have any unexpected complications, so we're gonna clear out of this place later today."

It was so strange, one moment he was sitting on his horse, sitting comfortably in his existentialism, the next he was panicking harshly. He didn't want them going back out on the streets where people could hurt them again. Suddenly the whole world was dangerous, with vile threats lurking around every corner.

They couldn't go out. Not yet. They needed more rest, especially Tawny. So, for the first time in ages, he lied.

"Oh, I was a bit frazzled when I checked you in and I used my points on top of paying for a week, so apparently I basically paid for two weeks."

"What, really? How did you swing that?"

"Believe it or not, it was a pretty stressful day."

"Okay, fair."

"But anyway, the days are already paid for and getting points refunded are an absolute pain. You might as well just stay there."

She was quiet again, and he swore he could almost hear her brain churning.

"Um, I don't know about that."

"I mean, you don't have to. But I'm certainly not going to stay there, and otherwise the room is just gonna sit there."

"I... this really seems like a lot."

His blood was pumping in his veins. He wasn't used to lying; he didn't like how it made him feel, but he couldn't think of another way to get her to stay.

He wanted her to say yes but didn't want to push too hard. "I mean, it's up to you, but I'm sure Tawny could use the extra rest."

"...yeah... I suppose."

He sat there quietly, waiting for her. He was beginning to understand why it was easy to take advantage of the poor. He had everything that both girls needed to survive. If he was nefarious, he could make their lives truly awful.

He wasn't, of course, or he didn't like to think that he was.

Frenchie continued, "Okay, but only if you let me cook you a meal. That is literally the absolute least I can do."

"Wait, you cook?"

Her sharp bark of laughter on the other end of the line was not expected. "Yeah, I cook. Try not to sound so shocked. I mean, it won't be anything fancy, but there's enough here in the kitchenette for me to make...something."

"You really don't have to." He didn't know what to say. It was strange to have a homeless girl cook for him. He didn't know why; he just knew that it was... strange.

She spoke up, "What's that thing you always say? Because I want to?"

He couldn't help the grin that pulled at the corner of his mouth. "All right, fine. Dinner and then you'll stay for the whole week. When do you want to do this?"

"Uh, it's still early, so how about tonight? That way, if you hate it, you can just kick us out."

"Yeah, that's definitely what I'll do."

"I knew it. The fate of the world relies on my culinary expertise."

"You know, I think I saw a movie about that."

"Hah, I'm sure you did. See you later, Solomon. After six?"

"Sure. Do you need me to get groceries?"

"No, I still have plenty of that money you slyly stuck into my pocket, don't worry about that. But since you're pretty enthusiastic, if you want to bring a dish to pass, that would be acceptable."

"All right, I'll see you at six then."

"Sounds like a plan. See you tonight."

She hung up and he stared at his phone, more pleased than he had any right to be. Whistling to himself, he finished up Maribella's walkabout then returned both horses to the stable, giving them a long, luxurious brushing then making sure he said 'hi' to every single other horse in the building.

By the time he made it back to his truck, it was nearly noon. Still plenty of time to cook something up. He wasn't a very good cook considering he always had either Mom or the house staff, but he could make a pretty mean chili. Usually he liked to let it slow cook overnight with braised beef in it and lamb fat, but five hours or so wouldn't be too bad.

So, he hurried home, a spring in his step. He was supposed to be working on something or another for his dad, but he'd taken the day off. It was his first vacation day in three years, and he wasn't mad about it. And, to be honest, it seemed like his father didn't even realize it. But that was probably because he was out golfing with his friends who all came from old money.

It felt good to be back in the kitchen, to be doing something with his hands. Grinning, he pulled his earbuds from his pocket, put on his music, and started his prep.

He was so engrossed in his activity that he didn't notice that his brother had entered until Sal was pulling one of his earbuds out. Solomon jumped, knocking his younger sibling's hand away.

"Geez, make some more noise, will ya? You almost gave me a heart attack."

But Sal just grinned like the occasionally annoying little

brother that he was. "Huh, you're in here cooking, but you're smiling. That's weird."

"Is it?" he asked, moving around his brother to continue what he was doing. Once he got everything into the slow cooker there wouldn't be much else for him to do, but he wanted to get it all in as fast as he could so it had the most time possible.

"Yeah, usually you're only in here after you get bad news, and you're almost always making brownies."

"Well, these definitely ain't brownies."

"Yeah, I got that. Looks like chili."

Something in his brother's tone made him cautious. "It is."

"What are you making it for?"

"I've got a dinner to go to." He didn't know why he was suddenly being so cagey, alarm bells going on in the back of his head.

"Oh really? With who?"

"No one you know."

"Really? You sure about that?"

"Why wouldn't I be?"

"Oh, I dunno. Just because I think it's with that homeless girl in the city."

Solomon actually choked on nothing, nearly dropping the spoon in his hand. For a brief moment he thought about lying, but he'd had far too much of that already in one day.

"It might be. It might not. Since when are you my keeper?"

"I'm not. But just be careful around girls like her, brother."

His temper spiked for a moment, white-hot behind his eyes. "What do you mean, girls like her?"

"Whoa, don't take it that way, man. But you know what Mom says. Sometimes people are so busy surviving that they forget how to be people. Remember that."

"Yeah, yeah, I'll make sure to do just that."

Sal shrugged and headed out, but inside, Solomon couldn't help but think that he had it all wrong. Frenchie's fight for survival made her more human than anyone in his own family was anymore.

But maybe, if he tried real hard, he could remember more of what it was like to be human too.

14

Frenchie

Frenchie couldn't remember a time when she'd been so well-rested, well-fed, and felt so completely safe. It wasn't going to be fun to go back out onto the streets, where it was cold and unsafe. Where she had to constantly look over her shoulder, be three steps ahead of life, and always have a Plan A, B, and C for everything.

Maybe that was Solomon's grand plan. To spoil her rotten until she was completely dependent on him, and then he would have her, hook, line, and sinker.

No, he wasn't that conniving. She had been tricked before, but never *that* bad. In fact, he pretty much seemed to be the exact opposite of that. All honesty, justice, and the rules. Heck, he probably dressed as Captain America on Halloween and tasted like apple pie if she kissed him.

Frenchie froze right in the middle of what she was doing, the cheap knife she'd found in one of the kitchenette drawers hovering over the cabbage.

Why was she thinking about kissing Solomon?

She shoved that thought out of her head as quickly as she could. She knew better than to get a crush on some rich guy. Life was not a fairy tale; she would not have some magical happy ending. Girls like her didn't get stories like that.

Shaking her head, she pulled herself back to reality and the matter at hand. Which was cooking a meal.

She was nervous, she had to admit. What she was making was limited by the pots and pans that were available in the little kitchen. She had a pot, a pan, a large skillet with high sides, and a couple of utensils. Sure, they were all battered, and she might have seen rust in the bottom of one, but it wasn't like she could invest in a good set, considering that she didn't normally have a kitchen to cook in at all.

So, she was making cabbage, rice, *tostones,* and grilled chicken breast. It wasn't the nicest thing that she could make, not by a wide margin, but that was all right. She had a feeling that Solomon would be able to tell how hard she tried anyway.

She finished cutting up the cabbage then put butter, salt and pepper into the bottom of the skillet and put it on low. She needed it to soften up a wee bit first before cranking the heat up, and she wasn't sure if the cracked lid was going to let too much steam and water out.

Oh well, it was the best she could do. She had learned to be skilled at being resourceful and using what was available to her.

Next was the rice, which was easy enough. She'd splurged, however, and gotten a little lemon and some lime juice to squeeze in for flavor.

She felt so blessed as she focused on the meal. Too lucky to keep everything to herself, so once everything was set on the stovetop, she turned to Tawny.

"Hey, do you think it would be taking advantage of Solomon's kindness if we invited a few of our friends over for this dinner? It feels wrong that we're sitting here all pretty while our friends are slumming it out there."

Tawny sat up from where she had been working in a math workbook that Frenchie had lucked out in finding at the thrift shop. "Dude, the guy who made sure you and me were set up here would definitely be all about you feeding the masses."

"Are you sure?" Frenchie studied her friend's face. The worst of her swelling was gone, but there were still deep yellow and green patches around her cheekbones and chin. She was going to need a tooth capped too, like she could ever afford that. "I don't want to seem ungrateful or like I'm using him."

"My girl, Frenchie, you are literally homeless and he's, like, a mega bagillionaire. He's not gonna care if you invite over other less fortunate folk to come and enjoy all this food you cooked."

"Well... all right. Maybe I'll call him—"

"Girl, why are you *bugging?* Aren't you the one who told me to take every opportunity I can?"

Frenchie wrinkled her nose. "I definitely didn't teach you that. Some opportunities aren't worth the risk, or have too much of a history of—"

"Gosh, okay fine, *Mom.* You taught me to always take advantage of every opportunity that wasn't a risk to myself and others. So, I don't know about you, but I'm going to go to the community center and invite a few people over for dinner. Except Ricky and Nancy. We don't need a fight starting."

"No, we definitely do not." She paled at the thought of

those particular people arriving. They were aggressive, to say the least, and she was pretty sure that they both had some pretty serious mental illnesses that were going completely untreated. Not that uncommon a thing in the older homeless folk. Especially considering that so many of them were veterans with PTSD. "All right, go, but if this goes sideways, I will totally throw you under the bus."

"Hah! Fair enough."

She took a minute to get up, and Frenchie couldn't help but feel a bit of worry as Tawny went to the door, but she told herself that she needed to calm down. They were both going to have to go back to the real world sometime, and she wouldn't be able to mother hen the young girl while she was out in the wild.

"See ya in a bit," Tawny said and headed out the door.

Frenchie nodded and turned back to the stove. She was tempted once more to call Solomon, but he was such a busy person and she didn't want to be annoying. She just hoped that Tawny was right.

Because, for some ridiculous reason that she couldn't quite say, she wanted to make him happy. At least for an hour or so. He had done so much for her and Tawny, and even though she couldn't understand why, she was still immensely grateful.

Because the change really was ridiculous. For the first time in weeks, her hands weren't chapped and every finger didn't have a hangnail. And as for her nails, they no longer were the flimsy, cracked messed they had been. In fact, they were almost solid and hard, something she'd resigned herself to never have again.

Every time she caught herself in the mirror, she saw that her cheeks were fuller and the dark circles under her eyes were a little less prominent. She had filled out so much for just one week, and she felt like her muscles were finally back again—even if she knew that probably wasn't physically possible.

Sleeping on a real bed did wonders for her; her spine didn't ache all the time and she wasn't constantly fighting off headaches or migraines. It was wonderful, it really was.

So maybe it wasn't so weird for her to want to make a really nice meal for the guy that had provided it all.

She was deep in thought as she cooked. Goodness, she must seem so stupid to him. She hadn't even graduated high school, and he was probably an ivy league graduate. He was the heir to a huge fortune and business, and she was... well, she was just Frenchie.

She didn't have too much time to get caught up in all of her inadequacies because then there was a knock on her door. She looked beside her to see that Tawny had left the hotel room key right where they usually kept it, so it could be her, or it could be anyone.

Carefully, she crept to the door and sure enough, it was Tawny with three others. She was surprised that the young girl had managed to rouse up a trio so late in the evening. Usually once the sun went down, everyone was off trying to find somewhere to sleep or get into a shelter in time.

She opened the door and greeted them to come in. She wasn't super close with them because they were too young for her crowd, but she'd helped all of them at one point or another.

There was Casey, who had been kicked out by his parents at the ripe old age of thirteen when they found out that he wasn't their little girl. There was Alitza, whose father had been deported while her mother was in the hospital being treated for cancer. Unfortunately, her mother never made it, leaving Alitza on her own. Finally, there was another one that Frenchie knew almost nothing about. He was a really tall guy with dark, dark skin and long dreads. He didn't speak at all, as far as she knew.

"Hey all, the meal will start soon. I did manage to buy drinks too." Sure, they were all the ninety-nine cent, off-brand two liters, but soda was a pretty rare treat for all of them.

She could practically hear their stomachs growling as they filed in, eyes wide. Clearly, they all had questions, but none of them asked how she or Tawny had managed to end up in such a nice suite. That was probably for the best. If they were doing anything illegal, the three young ones would at least have plausible deniability that they didn't know better. Besides, she knew what they assumed, and she didn't feel like it was worth it to dispel them of the notion.

She knew that some might be insulted by that, but she wasn't. Heck, she had thought the same thing at first, before Solomon had turned her down. And occasionally, if she thought too long about it, she would wonder if that was the case again.

Old habits were hard to break, it seemed.

She busied herself with cooking, but as she did, part of her began to wonder again if he had only turned her down because he didn't find her attractive. But that couldn't be the case, because he clearly did. Sometimes, the way he looked at her when he thought she wasn't looking, was so intense that she had to continue pretending that she was oblivious to his stare.

Ugh, she was a mess. This was all so confusing. She just needed to concentrate on dinner.

So that was exactly what she did, a low conversation starting with the four youngsters behind her. She could tell that they weren't being quite their usual selves, but she couldn't blame them for being a little tense. Even the offering of a free meal from one of their own was still a cause for slight suspicion.

But that was all right too, they could be suspicious on full stomachs.

Everything finished and she turned the tiny burners on the kitchenette stove onto low. Thankfully, she didn't have to wait long before there was another knock on the door and, sure enough, it was Solomon.

"Hey there," she said, smiling despite herself when she saw him.

"Hey," he answered, grinning just as much. He looked good, dressed in a black T-shirt and fitted blue jeans. She noticed that he was wearing cowboy boots, and they looked like they were actually used instead of being some sort of fashion statement. It was a *really* good look for him, all clean-cut and striking. With his high cheekbones and intense stare, he almost looked like the cover of a romance novel.

Minus the long, flowing hair and open shirt front.

"So apparently I am incapable of making a normal amount of chili. I made far too much."

"Oh, well that works out." She stood to the side, allowing him in. "Because we have company."

"Company?" he asked, striding in with a very heavy and very expensive looking slow cooker. It was clearly one of those super fancy ones that even came with a travel bag to keep it warm without scorching a table or car seat. Frenchie remembered her mother really lusting after one the last Christmas that they had as a family, but of course they couldn't afford that.

"Yes. I hope you don't mind. This is Casey, Alitza and, uh…"

"This is Alabama," Tawny said helpfully, gesturing to her friend. "He doesn't talk, but that's where he's from, so that's what we call him."

"I see. And all you young ones are…"

"Homeless?" Tawny said with a laugh. "Yessiree bob."

His face did that thing again, the expression he made whenever he didn't like what he was hearing but felt like he couldn't emote it without being rude. "I see. Well, let's get this meal going, shall we?"

"Sounds good to me," she said with a grin, going to the stove and starting to put things on plates. She knew that the kids wouldn't be comfortable serving themselves, caught up between the desire to eat as much as possible but also not being greedy and eating too much. The point of the meal wasn't to stress them out, so she had no problem handling it.

And to her surprise, Solomon went right into asking people what they wanted to drink and filling up the cheap cups from the little kitchenette. None of the cups matched, of course, but none of the kids were really in a position to care.

Not too long later, they were all sitting in a semicircle on the floor. There was a table in the room, but there were only two chairs, and it would be weird if two of them sat there while everybody else was on the floor. Solomon really had made a truly absurd amount of chili, but for some reason that tickled her all the way through.

But then she took a bite of it and she went from tickled right on up to *ecstatic.*

The chili was delicious. Mind-blowingly so. There was a sort of smokiness to it, and it was so *rich.* She eagerly took another bite, completely forgetting about her cabbage, rice and chicken breast.

"Is there... is there big chunks of meat in here?" Tawny asked loudly due to her excitement, her mouth crammed full of food.

Frenchie would have reprimanded her about manners, but she understood. She *absolutely* understood. The chili was *that* good.

"Normally I use braised beef in it, but I didn't have enough time so I used some of the pulled pork we always keep on hand. It's basically Sterling's favorite food and he eats it in about a million different ways. I browned the burger in lamb's fat too for flavor."

Tawny stared at him with wide eyes. "Wow, even your chili is a bagillionaire."

"What?"

Frenchie cleared her throat and handed her empty cup to Solomon. "Could I have a refill of the off-brand doctor, please?"

It worked, thankfully, and he seemed quite distracted. "Of course."

While his back was turned, she gave Tawny a look to *behave*, but she just giggled impishly around her mouthful of the delicious food.

"Eat your cabbage," Frenchie said finally.

"Sure, as soon as you do."

"I don't know why you don't want to eat it," Solomon said when he turned back. "This cabbage is *delicious*. And I don't even *like* cabbage."

"That's because most people just boil it until it's flavorless mush," Alitza said quietly.

"Well, I can't claim that I'm an expert in cooking it either, but good to know."

He was handling it so *well*. Maybe it was rude for Frenchie to be so surprised, but she couldn't help it. She was beginning to realize that maybe Tawny wasn't entirely correct that inviting three people wasn't a big deal—it was essentially throwing Solomon right into the thick of her world. A lot of people could look at older homeless folk and blame them for the situation that they were in, but it was hard to blame a child or teenager for being out on the street. After all, weren't parents and relatives supposed to protect them?

In Frenchie's experience, it hardly ever worked out that way.

As the meal went on, tongues went looser, and bellies got fuller. It was wonderful, and she felt all of them getting along.

"Oh, by the way, the cops over on the south side are getting really strict with the loitering stuff. Try not to be out and about during school hours or too late after dark. They picked up Imani last week, and as far as I know, they're hauling her home," Alitza said.

"Good luck with that," Tawny said with a snort. "Imani can get out of handcuffs faster than anyone I know. I put my money on her giving them the slip in a day."

"That'd be... what, the third time she's done that?" Casey said.

"Fourth."

"I take it Imani is a runaway?" Solomon asked.

For a moment Frenchie was worried that he was about to say something judgmental, but instead he just waited patiently for an answer.

"Yeah, she is," Casey answered cautiously.

"If she doesn't want to go to her home to the point that

she's escaping custody, why don't they help her find a foster family? Or an alternate living situation?"

"Because she's from New York. They don't have emancipation there so she's basically the property of her parents. They've been investigated by CPS, but unfortunately they can't do a lot about emotional abuse when all they have is a teenage girl's word."

Solomon frowned. "That doesn't sound right."

"And yet, that's how it is," Tawny said with a shrug. "She's only got another two years and then she'll age out. She'll be fine."

Casey sighed.

"Anyways," Tawny continued. "Did anyone see that the rich people department store is closing? They're having some mega sale, but I've still found a bunch of stuff in the dumpster out back."

"Really?" Alitza said.

"Yeah, they're throwing things out like crazy. There's some holes or snags on them, but I got a dress, a sweater, and a new bra."

"I'll have to check that out."

Frenchie noted some of their tips as they all exchanged information. Although she didn't need it at the moment, she wasn't going to be sitting cushy forever. In fact, she only had a week left.

The conversation continued until Alitza burped then let out a happy laugh. "Man, I feel like I won't have to eat for ages now. I am chock full of beans."

"I want that on record, because I'll put money on you complaining about being hungry tomorrow."

"You don't have any money, *Casey*."

"Yeah, yeah. Well, I might not have money, but I can tell

you that I heard the megachurch by the old community center just got a massive donation of food from some charity drive, from the parochial schools they ship all their rich kids off to."

"*No.*" Tawny's voice cut through the air, stopping the conversation right in its tracks.

"What do you mean, *no*?" Casey asked, laughing awkwardly. Everyone could sense that the air had changed and the young woman was sitting there, tensed like she was expecting an attack.

"I mean no. Don't go there. Don't go anywhere near there. Don't even look at it. It's not safe."

Sure, Tawny was a teenager and sometimes they could overexaggerate, but she knew that tone. She'd used it herself, in moments that she liked to bury in her memory to never look at again.

"Is there a reason why you're saying that, Tawny?" Frenchie asked.

"I...I..." Suddenly her face was in her hands and she was crying, big, wracking sobs that shook her entire frame. It was entirely unnerving, because she hadn't cried through the entire process, and before she knew it, Frenchie was up on her feet and moving to the girl, pulling her into her embrace.

"It's okay. We're right here. Just breathe for me, honey, *breathe.*"

"I-I *can't.*"

Frenchie had been around traumatized folks enough to know a panic attack when it was setting in. They were terrible things, cloying and filling the brain with thoughts that they were going to die.

"Yes, you can. Listen to my voice, okay? You're safe. You're with friends. Now in your head, I want you to list four things that you can see. Three things that you can feel. Two things that you can hear. One thing you can smell. Do that for me, okay? And breathe in and out the whole while."

The girl was as stiff as a board in Frenchie's grasp, but she could feel the young dancer's breathing slow down, backing away from that precipice bit by bit until she was only crying and not about to hyperventilate.

"Tha-that place is how I got messed up," she blurted out to the completely quiet room.

But Frenchie's stomach just about dropped out of her body.

"How do you mean, Tawn-tawn?"

"I was having a really bad streak of busking, just no one was shelling out, and I didn't want to dip into my savings. I'm so *close* to getting out of here, ya know?

"So I went there because I heard about the new fancy food center that they got. Nice stuff, stuff we don't normally get. And protein, lots of it. But when I went in, it was pretty late, and there was only one worker there. A guy. He said he was supposed to bring food to the door since it was late, but he made an exception for me because he could tell I was a good one."

She let out another wretched sob. "I'm so *stupid*, but I was just so *hungry*, so I went in with him. It seemed all right; he let me pick out whatever I wanted from the shelves. But then I tried to reach up for this jar of pickles that was up on a shelf and he was all pressed up against me."

It took all of Frenchie's willpower not to tighten her fists against the girl. That was the last thing that she needed.

"I pushed him off, and then he told me I was real pretty. He... he tried to solicit me, but I told him no. I pushed him away, but he didn't like that. So, he hit me, and then I fell, and then he wouldn't stop hitting me. I kicked him in the crotch to get away, and I barely made it."

She was crying again and Frenchie was reminded of just how young the girl was. "I'm so, so, sorry, Frenchie. I know you taught me better. But they really did have nice food. And I figured it was a church. Churches are supposed to be safe. Where is safe if that's not?"

"Hey girl, it's all right. It's not your fault you were tricked. He's the one who lied to you, who did something wrong. You're never in the wrong for believing in the good of humanity," Frenchie said.

Frenchie held her, rocking her back and forth, stroking her back. Her heart was aching, and her teeth were set against each other. She thought that she had learned not to waste her energy hating people she wouldn't see or crying about the injustice in the world, but she very much wanted to find the man and show him what it was like to be beaten to a pulp.

She was so wrapped up with Tawny and making sure she stayed tethered to the earth, that she completely forgot Solomon was there. Her eyes flicked to him, and the man looked like he was in utter shock.

Oh right, his family funded that megachurch.

"That... that can't be true," he practically whispered.

"I'm not lying!" Tawny cried, her tears kicking up again.

"Oh, no, no, I'm not saying you are!" He held up both of his hands, his eyes shuttling back and forth. "I believe you. I *believe* you. I just... I just don't know what to say. I never imagined..."

Frenchie knew that he wasn't arguing with them, but her temper spiked up a little anyway. "Like I said, you live in a different world from us. It's fine if you want to visit ours, you're nice enough, but you have to get used to the fact that this is how things are for us. Most of us can't go to the cops, so we're prime targets for being taken advantage of."

"I...I need to get some fresh air."

Suddenly he was standing then striding toward the door. Frenchie felt her heart ache as it closed behind him and his footsteps faded as he walked away.

Oh well. She had known that he couldn't last in her reality, where his privileges were shoved into his face on the regular. But still... he had been nice.

She was going to miss him.

15

———————

Solomon

*H*is mind was so full that it felt like it was going to burst, just explode into a million pieces and leave little shards of his thoughts all over the road as he raced home.

He hadn't meant to leave, hadn't meant to get into his truck, but it was like his body had taken over when his mind was utterly at a loss of what to do. When he came back to himself, he was already on the highway and headed towards home, knowing he needed to do *something* or he would explode before the night was over.

Not for the first time, he really pushed the speed limit as he went home. If he hurried, he would get there before nine thirty, which was when Dad usually started to wind down for bed. And once Solomon's father started his nightly ritual, there was no interrupting it unless there was a flood or tornado warning, and sometimes not even then.

And what was going on couldn't wait until morning. No, Solomon would lose it long before then. A girl had been beaten to nearly an inch of her life in the church that his family sponsored. The same church where he had attended the honorary dinner. The same church where he'd chased down Frenchie.

Out of nowhere, her interrupted art made more sense than ever. These kids were starving, scrounging around dumpsters for clothes, and ducking the cops to stay away from abusive homes, but they couldn't even go to a food pantry without risking being asked to pay for it in ways that they never should have.

It made him *burn* to think about it, and yet he felt like he could see it so clearly. Tawny was small and young. She must have been so terrified, trapped in some building, her food scattered across the floor as she tried to fight off some man that was twice her size. Had Solomon seen him at the dinner? Shaken his hand?!

He punched his steering wheel, resulting in a loud honk. He couldn't remember ever being so angry. He was known for his even keel and business sense, his poise and charm, but at the moment he felt like he was about to dive headfirst into the churning magma of his fury.

But he couldn't do that. Because that would be unproductive. No, he needed to get to Dad and explain the whole situation before another soul got hurt.

He pressed his foot harder to the gas. What if it happened again that night? Or the next day? Solomon had never given much thought to homeless people beyond the discomfort of them begging at exits to the highway, but that was before he had met a handful of them.

It was like he had been living in a world with blinders on and they had abruptly been yanked off, leaving him blinking at the light that he had been shielded from for so long. It just wasn't right, what was happening. It wasn't right at all.

He pulled his truck right up to their stupidly fancy drive at the front of the house, rushing in and tossing his keys on the counter. Either one of his brothers or the house staff would put it back in the garage where it belonged. That wasn't even close to important at the moment.

He had ten minutes or less to catch his father, and he sprinted towards the main wing of the house, which was where his parents usually spent their spare time. He wasn't sure where Dad would be, but guessing by the time, he was probably reading in his study.

He burst into the modest room to see that Dad was indeed there, nestled in his oversized recliner, a book in his lap and his special reading lamp behind him. His head jerked up at the intrusion, but other than that Dad was completely unphased.

"Can I help you?" he asked, his voice low and gravelly. He wasn't pleased.

Normally that was enough to make Solomon shore up and put himself into damage control mode, but he pushed through that instinct and walked right up to his father.

"I've found out some very troubling news about the church we sponsored the rebuilding of," he said all in one breath, trying to hold himself straight and tall. His father had taught him a million times over how posture could make or break a presentation, and as shallow as it sounded, he was certainly giving his father a presentation at the moment.

"Oh? Is this why you've been so distracted this past week or so?"

"Distracted? What, no. I mean, perhaps there's a correlation, but that doesn't matter at the moment."

Dad gave him a long, long look then shut the novel he had open, setting it to the side. Solomon noticed it was a biography of a fairly famous politician. If he recalled correctly, the man on the cover was related to the gentleman that Dad was hoping to get elected.

"And what is the matter at the moment?"

"The church runs a food pantry, one of the things we helped fund, but I've found out that a man there is using the food as a means to barter for sexual favors from the people who come there seeking help. And if they refuse him, he turns violent."

"I see." Dad's response was measured. Calm. It reminded Solomon of how he had been at first, the facts taking minutes to sink into his brain because they were so unfathomable. "And how did you find this out?"

"I spoke to a victim. And I know I can find more. I'm just worried about that taking too much time since these homeless young folks are scattered all around, and this man could hurt someone else while—"

Dad held up a hand, cutting Solomon off. "So, you've only talked to a single person, and I assume she was some homeless girl?"

Solomon didn't like how his father described Tawny. "I saw her injuries myself," he said. The conversation was not going as he expected.

"I'm sure you did. But unless you saw them happening, you don't really know why or how they happened." The older man yawned and stood. "The reality is, no one with any sense will believe a few homeless druggies who cry foul, so you should be able to make it quietly go away. The last thing we need is making a big to-do about it so the media can get all rabid with one of their witch-hunts."

Solomon just stared at the man, realizing that his father was telling him how to fix the situation to protect his own family and not the kids who were being hurt.

"What do you mean, make it go away quietly?"

He shrugged. "I've taught you well enough on how to handle the business side of things. Pay them off, have them sign NDAs, move the man to somewhere he will do less damage. Be smart; we paid enough for that college degree you didn't really need."

No.

No, that wasn't right.

Dad didn't want to help Tawny or Frenchie or any of them. He just wanted to do what was best for *business.*

"Dad, do you really think that our business goals are more important than protecting vulnerable people?"

"Vulnerable people?" Dad scoffed, already heading towards the door. "These folks put themselves into the situations they're in. Look at me, I started from nothing and because of hard work, we've got all of this."

"*Dad,*" Solomon heard himself hiss. "Your *parents* were rich and gave you all the money you needed to start this business. And their parents were rich before then. And their parents too. You're only here because you lucked out being born into a situation where you were safe, happy, and had all the money you could ask for."

Dad gave him a look over his shoulder, eyes narrowed in suspicion. "Who have you been talking to lately, boy? You're starting to sound like one of those far-left whackos."

Solomon could only stand there, torn between his shock and his anger. How *dare* he!? Dad didn't understand a single thing that these people went through. He didn't understand how *lucky* the entire Miller family was. That the things in their life were blessings, not something that they could boastingly take credit for.

"You have no idea what you're talking about," Solomon said with uncharacteristic boldness.

That stopped the man in the middle of his exit and he finally turned to fully face Solomon.

"What's going on? You're not turning into one of them snowflakes that demands everything be handed to them and sings kumbaya on some hippie commune, are you?" Dad said.

Solomon didn't even dignify that with a response. Finally, he understood why Frenchie said the things that she said about the rich, why she didn't trust anyone. He stormed past his father and went right back to his car.

No one had even had a chance to move it. Grabbing his keys, he found himself getting right back on the road. It took him a couple of minutes to even realize where he was going. He hadn't had a plan, yet he recognized that he was driving right back to the city.

To the hotel.

He was practically shaking with anger by the time he arrived, knocking on the door with a bit more force than he had intended. He should have known better; too aggressive of a knock would sound far too much like the cops for a room that was full of people who weren't exactly on the best terms with law enforcement.

But surprisingly, Frenchie did open the door. He saw that two of the three young ones were gone, but Alabama was sitting by Tawny's bed, gently wiping her tear-stained face with a cool cloth. There was an air of sadness but also of anger in the room, and he couldn't help but feel the same.

"I'm surprised to see you," Frenchie murmured, eyeing him warily.

"I'm sorry." The words were out of his mouth so fast that he almost interrupted her. "For everything. Every moment of everything. For chasing you, for not understanding all of this. For living thirty-three years of my life without doing a darn thing that would really fix any of this. I'm... I'm just so, so, *so* sorry."

"I..." She looked to him with wide, hazel eyes that quickly began to water. "I don't know what to say. It's not like you personally did this to me. It's just how the world is."

"But it shouldn't be. And I don't want it to be."

She wrapped her arms around herself, looking so helpless. Solomon felt that same compulsion to touch her, to comfort her that he had been ignoring for weeks, but it was beginning to be too much.

"Can I hug you?" he asked, voice thick.

She didn't speak, but she nodded emphatically. Then Solomon was striding forward with sure steps, wrapping his arms around her and applying what he hoped was enough pressure to be comforting but not uncomfortable.

And he just held her. Because if she was in his arms, then for at least a moment, she wasn't being hurt. She wasn't at risk. She was safe and sheltered, and he could keep all the bad things in the world at bay.

It felt far too right to have her in his gentle but firm hold, pressed up against him. He could feel her heart thundering against his middle, their height difference putting her head even with his shoulders. He wondered if she could hear his heart too, because it certainly seemed like it was racing off at its own behest.

They stood there for a while, probably too long, but he certainly wasn't going to be the one to push her away. So instead he kept holding her, living in the moment and only that moment, until she gently let her own arms fall to her side.

That was a clear a signal as any to let her go, so he did, taking a step away. "I know you all have so much on your plate, but do you all want to help me try to make our world at least a little bit better?"

16

———

Frenchie

*H*er heart was pounding, her hands were sweating, and she swore that every hair on the back of her neck was standing up along the goosebumps that pimpled her flesh.

She was nervous. Wait, no, scratch that, she was *terrified* as she approached the food pantry of the megachurch. It had taken a couple of days to get all the information they needed from Tawny, the poor girl had been so shaken up by the incident, and then another couple days to get everything they needed and also make sure that *that* man was working the night shift again. Apparently, volunteers were supposed to always leave by eight at the latest, but he was the only one who ended up staying until nine or ten, claiming that there was always "cleaning" or "sorting" to be done.

When Solomon had talked about helping, about making

the world a better place, she thought that he might haul them off to the police or some other foolish but honorable goal. But something must have happened because suddenly he was thinking like someone who lived in the real world.

He said that there was a chance that they wouldn't be believed, and that the evidence of one girl wasn't going to stand up in court. Not with his Dad and the other elite of the city closing in to protect one of their own. So, he suggested that they set up a bit of a trap.

Unfortunately, that meant Frenchie was the bait.

He hadn't liked that idea. Frenchie didn't like it either. But considering what they were doing, she wasn't going to put any of the young ones at risk. Besides, she knew how to hold down her own if worst came to worst.

...she just hoped it didn't.

Her feet felt like they weighed a million pounds each as she strode to the door. It was late, and she was there a half-hour after it was supposed to be closed. What was supposed to be a warm, inviting place was actually dark and looming, threatening her with several of her worst fears.

She pressed the button that looked like a doorbell and waited. She didn't hear anything, but Solomon told them that it was a lighted signal rather than a sound one.

She didn't know what she would do without Solomon being on the inside for them. He was the only one able to visit the church, which he did twice to learn little details that would help them with their plan. He was also the one who had supplied them with their equipment and a lot of the technical details they needed to succeed.

The door opened like she was in some sort of horror movie, and it was a tall, muscular man who answered. He was clean-cut, classic all-American, and he smiled brightly when he saw her.

"Hi, are you still open?" She forced her voice to be sweet and soft, an undercurrent of uncertainty layered in-between. "I'm sorry I was r-running late, I missed my bus and—"

The man waved his hand, all smiles and charm. "It's fine. Come right on in." He stepped to the side, allowing her to step past him, but as she did, his hand went to the small of her back to guide her.

If it were any other situation, Frenchie would have whipped around and slugged him in the face. But she couldn't. She could only smile at him nervously and let him lead her back around to the food.

And boy, Tawny hadn't been exaggerating just how much food there was. The room was at least as large as the suite, filled with shelves and shelves of nonperishable items. It was dazzling, and it actually would have been a very exciting moment if she wasn't full of so much dread.

"W-what can I take?" she asked, hoping the warble in her voice was believable.

"Whatever you want. Do you have access to a fridge and stove? We do have a few coolers."

"Yeah, I have a place I can go to cook once in a while."

"All right. Why don't you fill up that backpack you have?"

"Really? The whole backpack?" She had to hand it to the man, he was so sweet, so welcoming that she never would have guessed that he was capable of hurting someone like he hurt Tawny. But then again, she had known plenty of wolves in sheep's clothing during her twenty-three years. It was always the prettiest ones, the ones with the most honey in their voices and the most sparkles to their smile that were the most dangerous.

"Take as much as you need, love." His hand was still on her back, warm and heated yet promising things that made her blood run cold. "Probably need to put a little weight on, don't cha? Although you don't look so bad for being out on the street."

"I've had it lucky the past month."

"That so? Well that's good. I know a lot of the time all you guys can do is fill yourself up on junk and fast food. Makes you gain weight something terrible, so people don't take your hunger seriously."

Frenchie nodded. A lot of really poor kids and some of the homeless folk ended up getting puddly because all they could eat was cheap, junky stuff. Vegetables and fruit were a premium, leaving them with carbs, carbs, carbs. The only reason Frenchie was constantly losing weight was because she had a super-fast metabolism. Even when she was living in her home, she had always struggled to hold onto her muscle and weight, and that was with eating *all* the time.

...she missed having a doctor. She missed having *insurance.*

"Just take everything you need, all right? We're here to take care of you."

His words may have been meant to be comforting, but because she knew what he was capable of, they just made her shiver.

Hastily, she started shoving food into her backpack, hardly paying attention to what she was doing. Normally she would go for the highest calorie counts and the most filling, but her stomach felt like it was filled with spikes—not exactly the most appetizing of situations.

But if the man thought anything strange about her selections, he didn't say anything. No, he just walked along with her, his hand never leaving her back, occasionally sliding up her spine then back down.

It wasn't the first time she'd ever been in such a situation. If it was, well... she never would have been out on her own anyway. She knew that he was relishing his power over her, letting that invisible meter inside of himself build up until he felt the need to move onto the next step.

It was sick. Just because she was small, just because she was in need, he thought it gave him the right to demand things from her. From people like her. But she wasn't going to let him do it to anybody else. His hunting was going to stop with her.

But as determined as she was, her heart was pounding as her backpack was nearly full. It was time to make her move.

There, on an upper shelf, she saw some rice cereal. She'd always had an affinity for it, and it was just high enough that she was fairly certain the predator behind her would try the same thing that he had with Tawny.

"Oh, my favorite!" she said, trying to sound natural as she trotted over to it. As if she was excited and not caught somewhere between terrified and murderous. Standing on her tiptoes, she reached up for the box.

It was hard to keep her body movement normal, not to tense as tight as a bow as she went through her charade. And for a moment, time stretched impossibly, suspending her in the anticipation and fear of what he would do.

Then she felt it. His hand on her spine curled around one of her hips, his other hand going to the opposite so that he was gripping her tightly. She could feel the ten pinpricks of sharp pressure from his fingers digging in, letting her know in no uncertain terms that he wanted her to be still.

"W-what are you doing?" she asked breathlessly. She needed to get him to speak. To say his words out loud.

"Just helping you reach, sweetheart. Here, let me get that for you."

He took his time, one of his hands letting go of her to stretch above her head. She watched it, for the lack of a better thing to do, feeling his body press against her back much more tightly than necessary.

Even though she was wearing her hoody, it was like his slick, inky perversion was sliding across her flesh itself. Maybe even her soul. It always felt this way, when someone was trying to take something from her that she had no intention to give, and she found that it always left marks on her spirit that never quite faded.

Then, a moment or so later, it was done and he was stepping away.

"Let's go to the freezers, shall we?"

Frenchie nodded, feeling like she was going to swallow her tongue. She didn't really think she was a religious woman, but as she followed him into another room, she found herself internally asking for someone, maybe Jesus to help her. Or maybe for God to *do something* and smite his supposed servant who was looking at her like a wolf might look at a bunny naive enough to bounce into his den.

She let him corral her into a kitchen area, one wall being more like a counter at a diner where the workers could serve food to anybody visiting. It seemed that they were supposed to be giving hot meals to the community as well, judging by all the ovens and microwaves and tools, but she hadn't heard anything about that.

Her eyes automatically scanned the entire area, taking in any escape points she could find, logging them all in her mind to call on if she needed them.

Because she certainly had a feeling she would need them.

"Which freezer?"

Then it happened. He reached out to grip her wrist, not yanking her to him but definitely stopping her forward momentum. She looked to him, trying to affix a truly terrified look on her face—which didn't require much acting on her part.

"Yes?" she said.

"You know, I've been real nice to you letting you come in here after we're supposed to be closed. Don't you think you should thank me?" His thumb was moving in small, gentle circles on her wrist, but what the movement implied was anything but. "I could show you where they keep the real nice stuff. Jerky and steaks and all of that, if you were polite."

"Th-th-thank you," she whispered, trying to pull her hand away. "I appreciate it."

He pulled her a step closer, his front almost flush to hers. "I gotta admit, you don't seem like you mean it."

The shake that went through her body wasn't faked. "Y-you know what, I remember that I've got someplace to be. You can k-keep the food. I don't need it."

She went to slide her backpack off of her shoulder, pulling backward, but he just caught the strap with his other hand and shoved it right back into place.

"Come on, don't be like that. I don't like it when people lie to me. After I've been so nice to you?"

"I'm not lying!" she sputtered, trying to yank her wrist from his grip again. "Let me go!"

But he didn't, and she knew he wouldn't. Instead he jerked her until they were pressed right up against each other, his mouth right by her ear.

"What, you think you're too good for me?" Suddenly the "nice," charming parishioner was gone, leaving the man exactly as what he was: a monster in human skin. "Why is it so hard to just show a little gratitude?" He shook her harshly, and she allowed herself to be rattled. "Are you aiming to be punished? Is that it? Do you need the lesson beaten into you?"

He shoved her back and her hip collided with the counter, knocking her off-center. That allowed him to give a sharp shove to the middle of her back that sent her sprawling.

He stood over her, his foot coming down to pin her middle. She didn't even know his name, and yet she knew she was staring at her worst enemy. His hands went to his belt while hers balled into fists at her sides, waiting for the word.

"Your lot is so uppity, so arrogant," the man hissed. "You think you run the world, but you owe *everything* to us. So, you're going to be quiet, and then you're going to thank me for this, do you understand?"

She was frozen in place, wanting to tell him exactly what she thought of him and his tirade, but she couldn't. She had to be helpless against him until the signal sounded.

Just then, her earpiece crackled, and she heard Solomon's furious voice over the line.

"That's it! You have enough evidence, so get out of there *now,* Frenchie! We're already coming in."

Thank God.

Her hands went down to her middle, where his foot was pinning her in place. Gripping his toes and his heel, she quickly twisted his foot as violently to the side as she could.

He let out a curse and stumbled backward, limping, clutching the counter to hold himself up. His momentary surprise allowed Frenchie to crowd him, and she slugged him right across the face.

She'd never really been trained as a fighter but being as sporty as she was let her learn a bit about how the body worked, and then several sticky situations one right after another when she first was on her own was sort of a trial by fire. She learned that the last thing most attackers expected was for someone like her to press them, so the strategy was to rush them, get in the hits she could, then run for her life.

He shoved at her blindly, his hand flashing by her face, so she just bit it, chomping down with all of her might while her other fist punched at his throat. She missed, but that didn't matter because her mouth didn't, and perhaps she enjoyed the cry that rose from the man far too much.

He kicked at her, one of his big feet crashing into her thigh. She stumbled backward, knowing that there was going to be a bruise there in the morning, but she didn't care. As she crashed into one of the stoves, she reached above her to the hanging rack and grabbed a skillet, yanking it off the hook to slam into his face.

He reeled back. Frenchie was breathing hard, hyped up on adrenaline and survival, but she knew she had pressed her advantage as much as possible. She raced for the counter, vaulting over it and toward the front door.

She barely made it a couple steps when they burst wide open, Solomon having filched the keys the day before. Except he didn't filch so much as he told the church that his family wanted a copy of all the keys for their records and then had them make the full set for him.

But it wasn't Solomon who burst in, but Alabama and another one of the homeless folks she knew, Adam. It was, however, enough backup for her to feel less alone, less trapped, and she turned back towards the man. He was rising up to his feet again, holding his nose in vain against the blood pouring from it. She had probably broken it.

Good.

His eyes skidded from her to the other two men, and he realized it was *his* advantage that was gone.

As was true with almost any predator, he really was a coward. He turned on a dime and tried to run out of the other door, where there no doubt was a back section. He didn't make it far, however, because as soon as he threw the door open, he was tackled to the ground by none other than Solomon Miller.

"Let go of me!" the man cried. "This is assault!"

"Really?" Solomon snarled. "We have you recorded trying to sexually assault someone. We have the testimony and a medical report from the last girl you beat to a pulp. You're sunk, buddy. The cops are already on their way."

"You can't record me! That's illegal! This is a sanctuary!"

"Wrong, this is *my* family's property, and Texas has single party recording laws. My advice will be to lay there and shut up until you manage to get in contact with your no doubt sleazy lawyer."

"Your family?" The man craned his neck to look back at Solomon and went even paler.

Frenchie would have enjoyed his alarm, but she didn't think she could be satisfied while the man was still breathing.

"It's *you*," the predator said.

"Yeah, it's me."

"You don't understand, brother. I've been set—"

Solomon clapped his hand over the man's mouth, his anger quite evident. "Save it. I saw everything that happened through that little pin on her shirt—the pin that just so happens to be a camera. Like I said, just shut up before I do something decidedly unchristian."

It didn't seem possible that it could all be working out, and Frenchie found herself sort of detaching from what was happening. Nothing ever went right in her life. The bad guys never got caught, and they never had to pay for their sins. Yet that was what seemed to be happening right in front of her.

The cops didn't take long at all to get there. Much faster than they had ever reported to any emergency Frenchie had ever had. Then again, the crime they were reporting was happening inside of a multi-million-dollar church that was funded by one of the most elite families in the area.

It wasn't until the man was in cuffs and being taken away that Solomon came over to her, looking at her with that heady look again. "Are you all right?" he asked. His hands raised as if he wanted to touch her face, but they quickly dropped. "Did he hurt you?"

"No, I'm fine. My hip hurts a little, but that's it."

Solomon nodded. She could see his jaw moving as if he was swallowing several times, but before he could say anything, another officer was approaching them to take their statements.

The situation was still catching up to her, and Frenchie found herself not even caring about the *look* she got at telling the female officer she didn't have an ID or address. Normally she would huff up and tell them if they had a problem with it, they could give her a home, but she just didn't have it in her.

Besides, she didn't always need to put up a fight. A lady officer was more likely not to hassle her anyway, at least from her experience, so maybe it would be best not to have another enemy.

It was like someone had put a dampener on the world. All the voices became muffled. Frenchie just stood there, watching Solomon give his own report to another officer across the way.

He was mad; she could tell that. Even though they had won, and the guy was in cuffs and being put into a police car, Solomon was still agitated. Which meant that he *cared.* The situation affected him. He didn't hear about it and try to defend his church. He didn't feel bad and then dismiss it as something that was out of his hands. No, he heard about it and then did something about it. Not only *something*, but researched, made a plan, and went to action.

She was always suspicious, and the man that had just gotten arrested didn't help things. But... as she watched Solomon, she couldn't help but feel that he just might be legit.

If he was, that would have been the last thing she expected. What was that thing her *abuela* had said before she passed?

Oh, right. Angels could come in all sorts of forms. She just never figured it to be very true before.

17

Frenchie

*E*verything was just so *weird.*

It had taken them over an hour and a half before the cops let them all leave, the officers telling them that they would be contacted with more questions later. The cops hadn't been pleased when they found out that none of them had phone numbers beyond Solomon and the hotel, and the hotel stay was ending in just a few days. The best compromise the group could come up with was giving them the phone numbers of two of the local shelters they promised to stop by every few days.

And then they just... went home?

It was bizarre. And it was equally bizarre to wake up knowing that, for the first time in her life, she had helped to make someone pay for what they had done instead of just running away.

It was a good feeling, a real addictive one, and she began to wonder if maybe, just maybe, there was one iota of power and righteousness that she could grab onto and use to fight when these sorts of things happened.

"Huh, that really happened, didn't it?" She rolled over in bed to see Tawny's eyes open on the bed across from her. Her bruises were almost gone now, with only her two chipped teeth and the speckling in her eyes still being the most prominent signs of her injuries. "We really bagged him."

"He still has to be charged, and then there will be a trial, but Solomon said if they try to go easy on the guy that he's going to make sure that they don't."

"Sounds ominous. What does that mean? He's gonna go all vigilante on them?"

Frenchie laughed. "Hardly. I think he means to get his family's connections and mega-pants lawyers involved."

"Wow. Things really get done when you're loaded, huh?"

"Seems like it." Frenchie knew what the young girl meant. They all worked together in a web to protect each other, warning of people who hurt, who took advantage, who was to be trusted, because they'd learned along the way that no one cared what happened to them. But Solomon did care, Frenchie was almost sure of it now. And she was beginning to wonder how many of her beliefs were true, and how many were suspicions engrained into her by the worst of the worst.

And how in the heck was she supposed to find out?

"Whatever you did to that guy, I need to find me a rich man and do it too—because I was so certain I was dead for a while, but this has turned out to be two of the best weeks of my life in... what... ten years?"

"You're seventeen, Tawny, ten years is basically your whole life."

"Excuse you, it's only a little more than half. Don't give me that adult tone when you're only six years older than me."

Frenchie sat up, throwing her hair over her shoulder. "Six years is more than a third of your life. Don't sass at me."

Tawny let out an indignant sound and the next thing Frenchie knew, a pillow smacked her in the face. It fell away quickly, with both girls staring in surprise.

"Oh, my gosh," Tawny whispered, her smile growing. "I just hit you with a pillow. I basically started a pillow fight like a regular girl. I... why does this seem so important?"

"Well," Frenchie answered slowly. "It's important because you"—her fingers slowly curled around the edge of her own pillow, and then she was bringing it down on Tawny's head—"forgot to never drop your guard!"

The young girl let out a squeal as the pillow hit, and then it was on. Laughing, jumping around, the two of them were absolutely ridiculous as they bapped and bopped each other with the soft things. Frenchie knew it was a bit childish, but she didn't care. After everything that had happened, they deserved a little levity. A little nonsense. On the streets, there wasn't enough time for a pillow fight, or even pillows to fight with, and trying it in the shelters might result in being kicked out or banned. Something none of them could afford, but especially not the young ones.

It didn't last long, their little burst of activity, but after five or ten minutes the two of them were sitting on the floor across from each other—all of the pillows yanked off the bed— laughing and reminiscing about better and worse times.

Tawny was just in the middle of her story about begging her old doctor to remove her tonsils when the phone rang.

The sound was so abrupt, sharp and peeling, that both of them jumped. Frenchie knew only two people had their number, Solomon and the police officer woman, so she rushed to her feet to answer it.

"Hello?" she asked, trying to sound calm. In truth, she dreaded it being the police officer. Although the woman hadn't been the worst—heck, she hadn't even been that *bad*—Frenchie dreaded going into the station. Cops had never really been her friends her whole life.

When she was younger, it used to be they wouldn't believe her or let her file a report when she went in. She didn't have the right language to describe what was happening, and one of the higher-ups in the precinct was her stepdad's best friend going back to their military days. Later, when she'd tried to run away, cops were the ones who found her and returned her. And then she ran away again. It was the third time that she'd actually ever made it out of the city, and she'd had four close calls before she hit eighteen and finally didn't have to worry anymore.

But she still worried. It was hard to forget having her blood turn to ice anytime she saw a uniform. Vaguely, she knew that cops were supposed to help people and that they often did. That legally they had to return her to her parents and not all of them were out to hurt her. But it was so hard to separate that from the adrenaline and fear that spiked around them, and she was supposed to go to a whole *precinct* full of them.

Ugh. She really was messed up in the head, wasn't she?

"Frenchie! Were you up? I didn't wake you, did I?"

She let out a long breath when she realized it was Solomon, sounding concerned but pleased on the other end of the line.

"No, I was already up."

"You're breathless, is everything all right?"

She looked to the pillow still in one of her hands and

quickly dropped it, feeling herself flush. "Oh yeah, everything's fine. I just ran to the phone, is all." For some reason she didn't want him to know that she'd been doing something so silly. Something had shifted in how she thought about the man, and she found herself wanting to impress him.

She hadn't cared about impressing anyone in years. What was impressive about bathing in gas station sinks and having a sophomore education? Nothing. And yet she still wanted to try.

"Oh, all right. Listen, I wanted to get ahead of this thing, so I already pulled a couple of our lawyers onto this. Don't worry, they're the nice ones." He paused. "Or at least the nicest ones that we have who also have experience with the criminal justice world. Apparently, business law is an entirely different matter than civil law, which I think I knew, but I didn't ever think about, you know?"

"Uh-huh." What was the difference between business law and civil? She didn't know, but she wasn't going to admit to it over the phone to Solomon.

"But anyway, if you could gather up all the people who helped us out, I'd like to meet up with all of you later. I'll provide food, of course."

"Um... me n' Tawny could try. I know most of us are sticking around to keep an eye on each other, but I can't guarantee that we'll find them."

"Right... right, I forgot about the whole no phone thing. Do the best you can, and I'll swing by around... noon? Or would later work? Like, one? I do want to get all of you back before it gets dark."

"Okay. And the lawyers know that we're... that we're..." she trailed off, trying to think of how to say it in more graceful terms.

"That you're what?"

"You know... not fancy, like you and your family."

"They're aware that you're all in a vulnerable position, yeah."

"Okay. Cool, thank you." There was a sliver of relief but not that much. She still was going to have to meet up with some strange, intimidating lawyers, but at least they were warned ahead of time that a ragtag group of ne'er-do-wells was about to invade their lives.

"Why?"

Again, she really didn't want him knowing that she was worried about what they thought of her, and by extension, what he thought of her. "I dunno. Just seemed important. But later would be better. Sometimes we tend to gather after the lunch rush just by coincidence, so I stand a good chance of rounding them all up."

"All right then, noted. See you then."

"Sounds good."

He hung up and she set down the phone receiver, reminding her of *Abuela's* old landline when she was younger.

"So, what's the deal?" Tawny asked, flopping back on her bed and looking at Frenchie. "What about after lunch?"

"We need to go round up the others. Get your shoes on."

"Oh geez. That sounds serious."

"It is. We're going to meet up with some of Solomon's lawyers."

"Ew, gross. That won't be the easiest sale to the others, you know."

"Solomon also said he would be providing food."

"Oh, and there you go. I'm up!"

True to her word, she jumped to her feet and went towards her shoes. Frenchie chuckled to herself, although when she thought about that delicious chili that Solomon had made, she realized that yeah, it would be easy to get everyone to agree to go if she found them.

She just had to actually find them first.

IT WAS BASICALLY A CHRISTMAS MIRACLE, because after three hours of pounding the pavement and then going to the community center, she had found Casey and Alabama, with several others promising to get word to Alitza, Adam, and Chantal. Frenchie was especially grateful to the latter two, who hadn't been around for Tawny's revelation, but apparently were good friends of Alitza who she knew would want to help. There was more of a story there, something about a mechanic, but there hadn't been time for the whole thing to get explained out. All that Frenchie knew was that the duo had come when their friend called and helped out immensely with their little sting operation.

"So, did he say what he was going to make?" Casey asked as they walked back to their hotel. "More chili? Pizza dipped in gold?"

"I don't think gold pizza would taste very good," Adam said with his thick southern accent. The boy was from all the way deep down in Louisiana. He had a drawl that was difficult for even her to discern sometimes, and she'd been in the south for years. "Although I hear it's real malleable, so maybe ya wouldn't break your teeth."

"What's that mean?" Tawny asked. "Mall-able?"

"Mal-e-able," Adam said. "And it means, uh, able to be molded, I think? Like kinda soft, even if it's metal."

"Ahhh, *malleable.* That's a good word."

Frenchie already knew the word, but it pleased her that Tawny was expanding her vocabulary. She was acutely aware that knowledge was power, and since none of them had finished high school, they had to grab whatever they could whenever they could.

She knew she wasn't *stupid*, per se. None of them really were. But it bothered her that there were whole chunks of knowledge missing from their experiences as humans. Back before the old library had been 'dozed, she used to go there all the time in the extreme heat and extreme cold of the winter so she could curl up with a book or hop onto their computers. She learned *so* much from the internet.

Maybe, after she was done with the lawyer business, she would ask Solomon to stop somewhere she could grab a post-card and stamps, then she could mail something to herself for proof of address. That didn't solve her ID problem, but the last time, she'd emailed the library a picture of her old ID, and that had been good enough. It was still saved to the email host cloud, and maaaaaybe it wouldn't matter that it was expired?

It gave her a sliver of hope, and that hope only brightened when they approached the hotel and spotted Alitza and Chantal outside of it.

"We heard you were looking for us?"

Frenchie nodded. "Yeah, Solomon wants us to meet up with his lawyers."

Alitza wrinkled her nose. "Really, you called us away from the best day to dumpster dive at the mall to meet with a bunch of suits?"

"He also said he was providing food."

"*Chica,* why didn't you start off with that? When do we head out?"

"Just an hour or so from now, I'll have to check the time. But first I want all of us to shower."

"Why's that?" Adam drawled. "You saying we smell?"

"Absolutely." Frenchie flashed him a grin as she slid their keycard through the door and opened it. "And we don't want these lawyers doing a bad job if they can't breathe."

"Man, I wish I had some clean clothes," Alitza grumbled. "We were just in the dumpsters. Even if we take a shower, we're not exactly going to be smelling like roses."

"Hmm, I can go grab some towels from the front desk and... lemme see." She craned her neck towards the clock. "It's twelve fifteen, so I think I can probably run them down to the laundry and get them clean and dry in time. Everyone okay with that?"

There was a chorus of agreement, so Frenchie went about the whole process of making sure that everyone had enough towels to be decent if they were worried, then collected their clothing.

She had no problem spending the four dollars that were needed to put the dirty clothes in the washer, buy the detergent, then put them in the dryer. She was grateful that the laundry was connected to the lobby, because she could leave it safely while she went back to the room and did several other things. Such as brushing her teeth in the kitchenette sink and brushing her hair.

Her roots were *really* grown in. She only managed to dye it every once in a while. She would go to the local beauty school and volunteer for them to do whatever they wanted short of shaving her bald, but she hadn't had a chance to go there lately. She wished she did, because she looked a little rough.

Or a lot rough.

Her skin was splotchy, and even with two full weeks of really spoiled living, her body was just... strange. Her muscles, along with some fullness, were coming back in her arms and her calves, but her stomach was still mostly concave and all of her ribs showed. She hated it. She missed how she used to look, happy and healthy and full of energy. Maybe, if she could have been that girl for longer, she could have grown into a woman that Solomon could be interested in.

Right, and maybe unicorns existed too.

Besides, what did it matter? She knew that daydreaming about things that could never happen was just depressing, and why should she *care* what kind of woman Solomon would like. As she had said and thought many times, he lived in an entirely different world than her, one that she couldn't even touch. And although he was a wonderful visitor, there was no way he'd want to pull himself down into the muck by lowering himself to her level.

Ugh. She just wished she didn't keep thinking of how he sounded when he had told that man off. Or how he looked at her. Or the strong line of his jaw whenever he pressed his lips together in thought. Or how long his lashes were (*unfairly* long), or—

"Hey, are these socks up for grabs?" Alitza asked, interrupting her thoughts. "Because I could really use a new pair."

"Yeah, of course," she answered, shoving all thoughts of Solomon away. "Help yourself to anything. There's food too."

"What, really? Wow, you guys got it good up here." The girl did indeed start helping herself, which made Frenchie feel better. "What, you like his sugar baby or something?"

"No, nothing like that."

The girl squinted at her. "Really? But people just don't usually do all this without expecting something back."

"You know, I used to think the same thing."

"And you think you've changed on that view?"

"Maybe. I think so."

"Huh, maybe I should get me a rich not-sugar daddy and see if I change my mind too."

Frenchie huffed and threw an empty bag at the girl before returning to her tasks. The time flew by, and before she knew it, Solomon was knocking at the door.

She rushed over, pausing just before to smooth her hair and then opening the door only a crack.

"Hey, sorry I'm about ten minutes late, it took me longer than I expected to navigate through the city with the van."

"Van?" she asked, not sure she heard right.

"Yeah, we certainly weren't all going to squeeze into my car. You all ready? Did you get everyone?"

"Yeah, I did, but we need about, uh, ten more minutes for their clothes to dry downstairs. We didn't want to show up all stinky, but I forgot how slow the machines are here." That was a mild lie. She had forgotten how long washers and dryers took in general, but she didn't want Solomon to think she went around dirty all the time. She worked hard to keep herself as clean as she could, that routine just didn't usually include functional appliances.

Solomon's eyebrows furrowed just a bit, giving him a serious look. "Frenchie, if you're worried about them saying something, they wou—"

"So yeah, just about ten minutes. You want to walk to get a soda at the vending machine with me? I feel like splurging."

"A soda from a vending machine is splurging?"

She nodded as she pushed past him, feeling a bit prideful that her guess had been exactly right on how to distract him. "It is when soda from the store is ninety-nine cents and water fountains are free. Come on, walk with me, then we can grab the clothes."

"Whatever you say."

Coming from someone else, that might have been conde-scending. But from Solomon it was anything but. She got the impression that he was used to being in charge of things, of calling the shots and managing meetings and whatever else the heir of an empire needed to do. But with her, he deferred more often than not. Either he trusted her, or he was the most easy-going business shark she'd ever met.

"So, how do you feel?" he asked.

Frenchie shot him a curious expression as she bent down to get her soda. She'd tried to pay with her own money, but Solomon had used his long arms to slide his card through the machine before she even had a chance. Back when she was a little kid, vending machines wouldn't take cards and she'd never owned one herself, so she'd been so surprised she'd just stared at it for a few moments.

"What do you mean?" Frenchie asked.

"I know there are more bad guys out there, but you managed to help stop one of them."

"I didn't stop him. *We* did. We couldn't have done it without you."

Solomon shrugged, his broad shoulders catching her atten-tion in a way they probably shouldn't. "I don't need the credit. I should have been doing way more for years. I always thought we were ahead of the curve because we donated so much to charity, but looking back..."

He grimaced, and for some bizarre reason she wanted to reach up and stroke his face. She was sure he wouldn't appre-ciate that.

He continued, "But I don't think that a single one wasn't somehow to benefit us. There were tax write-offs, the alliances, the political favors my father was trying to curry. The things he said about people in need... I don't want to get into it, but it made me think about some things."

"Oh?" She didn't know what to say to that. She wasn't surprised his father was less than kind, but it was strange to hear that he was questioning things. People rarely shook their biases, especially when they were handed down by their folks.

"Yeah. But I can't really dedicate a ton of time to it until this is all cleared up. I'm trying to make sure his bail is ridiculously high. I don't want him out and about on the streets or getting away."

She nodded. She was past the point of asking him why all the time, even if she still wondered it in the back of her head. "That's smart. You seem to be on top of this."

"Yeah, I used the spare time I had when we were setting the trap to research as much as I could. I wanted to make sure we didn't get him arrested just for him to walk away."

"I really appreciate that." The words didn't seem to be enough, but that was all that she could do. She had nothing to give him, and she wasn't smart enough to teach him anything. It wasn't like he needed street smarts or anything like that. So much of her brain was dedicated to survival and protection that there wasn't much room for anything else.

"Think the clothes are done now?" Solomon asked, clearly changing the subject. But she was grateful for that.

"Let's go check."

They went down to the laundry room and there were a couple of minutes left, so they mostly just stood around. Frenchie felt acutely aware of Solomon's presence and how he stood, his posture, the timbre of his voice. The laundry finished quickly, and he insisted on carrying it upstairs.

She allowed him, but once they got to the door, she took the clothing and slipped in. From there, the boys changed in the bathroom, and the girls in the bedroom, before they all were heading right back out.

She remembered Solomon mentioned something about it taking an hour to drive there and back, so she settled in for the ride.

"Everyone buckled in?" Solomon asked once all of the doors were closed.

"Wait, do we really?" Tawny asked.

"If you want this van to go, then you bet. You didn't spend two weeks recovering just to end up thrown out of the windshield if anything happens? So buckle up."

"All right, all right, Daddy Warbucks, breathe a moment."

Frenchie shot the young girl a look in the rearview mirror. Tawny just batted her eyes. Cheeky.

"Anyone have any objections to some music?" Solomon asked.

"I don't think any of us are in the position to tell you what to do with your car," Frenchie answered. "And by the way, since when do you have a van?"

"I personally don't. This is one of the work vans. Figured no one would miss it. Anyway, I've been listening to some Celtic music lately. Let me know if you absolutely hate it."

"Frenchie won't," Tawny continued blithely. "She loves music and listens to it all the time. Her MP3 player is the most valuable thing she owns."

"It's a really good one," Frenchie said with a shrug. "It was fifty dollars when I got it five years ago, on clearance, and it's lasted ever since. Battery goes for two or three days even though I listen to it for ten hours at least out of the day."

"That's impressive. I always hate transferring music onto a new phone."

"Remember when phones and music players used to be

separate devices?" Frenchie said with a smile, leaning her head against the window. With the rumble of the engine, she was starting to get sleepy. She had forgotten that cars were great at putting her right to sleep.

"Uh, no," Casey said from the back. "That sounds like fake news."

"No, it's true," Adam followed up. "I'm a couple years older than you, but I remember my older sis used to have a flip phone and an MP3 player when I was a li'l one, and I was so jealous."

"Wait," Solomon said. "Are any of you over twenty?"

"I'll be twenty-one in a couple months," Chantal said quietly. "Adams four months or so older than me."

"I see."

"Why?" Frenchie asked, cracking her eyes open to glance at him. "Did you buy alcohol?"

"No," he said with a laugh. "Just curious, I guess."

"Well, you know what curiosity did to the cat," she yawned, leaning her head against the window.

"I've heard, but did you know that satisfaction brought it back?"

"Huh?" she was so warm, so content, that it was hard to hold onto what he was saying. "No, I didn't know that."

"Well, it's something to think about."

"Mmhmm, something to think..." But then she was slipping under, feeling so cozy that it was easy to forget everything else.

18

———

Frenchie

"Wow, even the air is different out here," Alitza said as they stepped out of the van. "It reminds me of when Papa used to work on a farm."

Frenchie slid out of the van, yawning and stretching her arms. She was surprised to see they were in some sort of warehouse-like area, more tall buildings and silos rather than the opulence that she expected.

"Is... this the ranch?"

"What, this?" He laughed softly, but it wasn't unkind. "This is just a garage, repair shop, and the tool sheds. Oh, and the silos. I guess. They're the old ones, though, so they're mostly filled with junk. I figure we could ride in my pickup truck to the estate since we won't be going over the highway or anything like that."

The estate? Tawny mouthed to Frenchie, but she just

shrugged. They would see it when they saw it, and that would be that.

Or at least that was what she told herself. But as they clambered into the back of a fancy-looking and oversized pickup truck, she couldn't help it as her head swiveled back and forth.

She couldn't see much until they pulled out from the garage area, and then she was just as shocked as she told herself not to be. There was just so much *space!* And there were fields as far as she could see, some green, some white, some tan. Some of them waved in the breeze, but they were all so *pretty.*

Alitza was right, even the air was better, and she drew deep drafts of it into her lungs. She felt energized and strangely alive. Connected to the earth in a way she hadn't in a long time.

"Oh my goodness! Look at all those cows!" Tawny said.

Frenchie followed Tawny's pointed finger to see lots of cattle roaming in a field a bit in the distance. They were bigger than she expected them to be, even from far away, and she wondered what it would feel like to pet one. Maybe, if things worked out, she could ask Solomon to let her see them up close.

...if he still wanted her around. What if they finished up all of this court stuff and he moved on? Clearly, she wasn't going to be some sort of staple in his life. She was a no-account street kid who had grown up into a no-account street woman and didn't even have a GED to her name.

She tucked those thoughts away and just enjoyed the moment. Even though there was a cold bite to the air, and that was only amplified by them driving along, it wasn't oppressive. Then again, that could be because there was a blanket spread across the back and another for them to all huddle under while the young ones and Frenchie looked around.

It was beautiful. There was no denying that. It was completely different from the city. She didn't understand why Solomon would ever want to leave it. If she could just be surrounded by plants and open space all the time, she would be content.

But the real question is, were there any horses? Her hands were itching to draw a horse. Or lots of them. All long legs and flowing manes. The Millers were rich, weren't they? Which meant they had to have some mounts around. Equestrianism and wealth went practically hand in hand.

She was so busy scanning for horses out in the field that she wasn't paying attention to where they were going. Or at least, she wasn't until she heard a shocked gasp beside her.

"No way, is that his *house!*?"

She turned around and looked where Tawny was pointing yet again, and her jaw dropped. The mansion she was seeing was like something out of a Hollywood movie, big and sprawling with at least three stories and spread out way too far to be possible.

"How many people must live there?" Alitza whispered, just as awed, and Frenchie couldn't blame her.

The house was just so *big*. Impossibly so, and yet the closer the pickup truck drove, it got even bigger and bigger until it was unbelievable. Like something out of a cartoon, it was so ridiculously large that Frenchie had to rub her eyes to see if she was hallucinating.

There was a full fountain up front and a massive drive that a whole carnival could probably set up in. Who had a fountain that was at least two people tall in the middle of Texas? How much must their utility bill be?

Perhaps it was a silly thing to think about, but her mind was scrambled as she looked up at the yards and yards of real estate. The building was a sort of classic glamour, with pillars up front and several balconies. The roof was covered in what she recognized as those super fancy solar panels that she saw on the news, and there was a pond on the left side of the building. And by pond, she meant a large, clear body of water that had a dock attached to it for people to jump off of during the hazy summer days when they wanted a cool swim.

Wow. Being rich was crazy.

Solomon pulled right up to the front door, which was made of beautiful, intricately carved wood. Stained glass sat in the middle of each panel then around the edges, casting a beautiful prism of light across the stone porch.

Her hands itched to draw again. Being surrounded by entirely new things and such grandeur made her want to sketch it all, as if to prove that it was real and not some figment of her imagination.

"All right, everyone in," Solomon said, getting out of the front of the truck. "Meet with the lawyers first, and then you all can eat."

"Question," Adam asked as they all piled out. "If you were just gonna haul us here with a truck, why not just use the van? Not that I'm complaining."

"Because the van belongs to the company and if I leave it out here, one of our house staff will return it to the garage since that's our policy. This, however, is my brother's truck, so they'll park it in the family's personal garage, which will be much more convenient."

"Wait, you guys have two garages?"

Solomon gave them a surprised look, as if he didn't think that was all that special, before he nodded. "I'll give you the full tour of everything once business is taken care of. Now come on, I'll get y'all something to drink while you're talking to the legal folks."

Oh right. She had been so swept up in everything that she had forgotten the reason that she was actually there. Trundling inside, she felt the seriousness of the situation start to sink in, but it was instantly banished once she looked up and saw everything that was inside.

"Is that a *chandelier?*" Casey asked. "In your *house!?*"

"Technically this is my parents' house, but we all live here. Most of us have our own wings or floors, but the twins share one. They're not as close as you hear about most twins, but they're still quite a pair."

"Wait, your brothers are—Oh, what's this?" Tawny was pointing to something in the wall that Frenchie couldn't even identify. It looked like a TV or computer screen, except it was dark and completely set into the wall.

"Oh, that's just one of the housing interfaces. You can lower the lights or change the heat and AC or even see who's home. Check our schedules that we all put on their too."

"Whoa, bro, are you telling me your house is *literally* a computer?"

Solomon heaved a sigh, but it was a good-natured one. "This is going to take a minute, isn't it?"

Frenchie nodded, trying to hold back both her amusement and curiosity and failing at about eighty percent of that. "I think we might be a little late."

FRENCHIE HAD no idea how Solomon managed to corral all the young ones into a meeting room, but after fifteen minutes of ushering, they all somehow ended up inside and in chairs. She also didn't know what an actual meeting room had any business doing in a house, but considering how big the place was, maybe they just had one of everything lying about.

It was so bizarre seeing how the other side lived. Solomon could fit three of the public libraries inside and still have room to throw a party. She knew he had a big family, something like five brothers, but how did they live with so much space? Sure, she liked driving around the countryside, but that was different than living a mile away from his roommates.

Except they weren't his roommates, they were his family, which made it all kinda sad.

She didn't have time to dwell on that, however, because then the lawyers were introducing themselves and two new people, who were apparently their criminal law contacts from inside the city. Things got really serious then, with them asking lots of questions and telling each of them the possible roadblocks and curves that might be thrown at them. The man who had assaulted Tawny and attempted to assault Frenchie came from a very rich family, and they were throwing their everything into protecting him. The lawyers told them that the defense would spend a lot of time and effort into mischaracterizing them and tearing apart their character and that they needed to be prepared for that.

Of course, that caused its own conversation when Tawny and Alitza both got worried about testifying. One, because Tawny was afraid her family would sweep in and cart her back home when she was just a few months away from being eighteen. And Alitza because she was afraid they would deport her like other members of her family even though she had been born in the United States. It took a while to sort that out, and in the end, Alitza apologized and said she couldn't risk it. There were horror stories all over of people being snatched up and held for weeks, and she didn't have any ID to prove her citizenship, so it took the lawyers agreeing to set up a witness protection of sorts for her. Frenchie wasn't entirely sure what it entailed, but it involved her being in a safe house and having escorts to and from the court when the time came.

That went better than Frenchie thought. At least that would get her off the streets for the worst of the winter.

All in all, it was at least two hours before the lawyers said they had all they needed, and they also mentioned that they would want to meet again in a couple weeks. The trial likely wasn't even going to start until spring, and the lawyers were hoping to do a sort of plea deal that would maybe keep them from ever having to go to court at all.

When they finished, Solomon led them down to the kitchen where there was a veritable *feast* laid out, a woman and a man in black and white uniforms working on putting out more. There were thick sandwiches with big portions of meat between the soft bread. There were chips and dips of several types. There were fresh vegetables and a fruit platter with also three kinds of dip for that. Frenchie didn't even know there was such a thing as dip for fruit!

There was also a big pan full of messy, saucy, absolutely delicious pulled pork, spare buns, and fresh greens.

"Holy cow, Solomon," Frenchie gasped. "You really weren't kidding about the food."

"Heck, if you're gonna feed us like this every time," Tawny said, skittering forward. "Then I'll come here and talk to a bunch of lawyers whenever you want."

"Same here," Casey said, rushing forward. "This is legit."

Everyone busied themselves with getting food, and Frenchie only realized just then how hungry she was. Apparently, her body had gotten used to eating on a fairly consistent schedule. That was going to suck when things went back to normal. At least she had managed to send her resume into several shops that were likely looking for seasonal work.

"Eat as much as you like. I'll have the staff pack up what you don't finish and send it with Frenchie so she can keep it in the fridge at the hotel. You all can pop by there whenever you want more food."

"Oh, so then you don't mind if we have people over at the hotel?" Frenchie asked.

"What? No. Why would I mind?"

"Well, because it's your place, technically. We didn't want you to think we were taking advantage by having people in and out whenever we wanted."

But Solomon just shrugged, surprising her. "I trust you to use it however you need. Whoever can stay there as long as they don't damage things. Especially since it's getting colder."

"All right then. That's good to know." She took a bite of her sandwich that she had just picked up and then flashed him a closed-lip smile.

"Of course."

"Oh man, this food is *good!*"

That broke the strange, sudden intensity between the two of them, and soon everyone's attention was turned to the food. It really was delicious, and it was only mildly weird that it was made by two people who didn't join them for the meal at all. Frenchie had never met a maid or butler in real life, and it was something she'd assumed she'd never get to experience.

Nevertheless, the meal went along swimmingly, and it wasn't long before everyone was sitting along the island in the middle of the room, leaning back in their chair and holding their bellies.

"Oh man, I'm so stuffed," Adam said, stretching lazily. "Do

we have to go right back? Cause I think I might pass out in the back of your truck there."

Solomon looked pensive a moment, rubbing his chin with his hand before he seemed to suddenly make up his mind. "Actually, why don't you all take some naps in the guest rooms? I'm sure you could use the rest."

The suggestion warmed Frenchie's heart, and all of the young ones outside of Tawny shared surprised glances, but then the logic came swinging in. "What about your father? Didn't you say he... wasn't a fan of us?"

But Solomon just shrugged. "He rarely comes into my wing, and if he does, what is he going to do? I'm a grown man, and I'm the only one who can run the entire business in his retirement. If he wants to play hardball, I'm the worst person to do it with."

Frenchie had about a million and one other things to say, and yet somehow, she couldn't articulate any of them. She wanted to thank him, wanted to tell him that he was ridiculous to put them before his family. Wanted to say that he couldn't change anything no matter how hard he tried, and yet even another that wanted to cry just because he *cared*.

But instead she stayed quiet and let him lead them far away from the kitchen. Her alarm spiked again at leaving such a mess, but then she saw the same two house staff members slipping in to organize things.

Wild.

It was a surprisingly long trek to his wing and the guest bedrooms, which he had four of, which they didn't even use up, as half of them had two beds instead of just one, and most of the young ones preferred to sleep curled up together.

Frenchie understood why. In the winter, warmth was the hardest commodity to come by, so most of them would crash together at night if they couldn't find a shelter to stay in. It was a sort of creature comfort, one that came from thousands of years of being a pack animal.

"What about you?" Solomon asked when everyone was eagerly getting into bed and settling down. "You ready for a nap?"

Frenchie shook her head and let out a small laugh. "No, I napped in the car."

"Well, in that case, want to go on a bit of a walk?"

"Oh, sure. Why not. You gonna take me on a tour?"

"Maybe something a little less formal. It's not that bad of a day outside. Maybe we could see the chicken coup?"

"You have chickens here?"

"Not professionally, but Mom likes them a lot, so we got maybe fifteen or so. Rare ones too."

"There are rare sorts of chickens?"

He laughed. "Oh man, are you in for a treat."

"Am I?"

He didn't even seem to think twice as he took her hand in his and led her to a different staircase. She didn't say anything either, but she felt her whole body flush with heat and her heart start to beat as hard as it had when she was in the chase he gave her when they first met.

Oh boy. She was in so much trouble.

She tried to push the thoughts away, but they all swirled around her head as he led her outside. It wasn't until the cold hit them and he went to zip up his jacket that he seemed to realize how he had been holding her.

"Sorry about that. I didn't even realize."

"It's fine," she answered quickly. Except it wasn't fine. She was beginning to feel things that she wasn't supposed to feel. Think things that she shouldn't think about. In her situation it was dangerous to want things outside of the most basic needed for survival, and even that was tricky.

"Right, well, this way then."

She nodded and followed along after him, doing her usual two and a half steps to his one long stride, and soon they came across a pretty little mock cabin.

"Wait, is this seriously where the chickens live?"

"You know, all of you use this same tone when questioning my life, and it's going to give me a complex."

"Well, we can't help it that your life is a little ridiculous." She looked at the structure in front of her. It was taller than her, but mostly because it was raised, with a set of three long steps going up to the front that was a chicken-wire covered gate. "This is the size of some people's apartments."

"What, no it isn't."

Frenchie fixed him with her most serious stare. "Yes, Solomon, it absolutely is."

He shook his head, undoing the latch and holding it open for her. She skipped past him, slowing down once she was fully inside.

"Wow, these chickens are pretty! And... kinda weird looking."

"Yeah, designer chickens can be a little bizarre."

She stopped again and gave him a look. "Are you telling me that you guys are so rich that even your chickens are designer? They're *birds*."

"You know, I never used to think about how many of the things I take for granted are rich people things, but now I wonder if anything about my life is normal."

She laughed at that. He was taking everything remarkably well. "Well, I'm sure y'all drink water from the tap just like the rest of us."

A strange expression crossed his face, followed by a sharp, short laugh. "Actually, we have a filtering system in our fridge and it comes out of the door."

"Oh my gosh, really? That's... I don't know, do you at least put on your own underwear? That's the only other thing that I can think of."

"Well you can rest assured that I have been putting on my own briefs since I was young enough to know what they were."

"There you go. That's the one common unifier. We all put on our underwear. Such a strong connection."

"Well, it's a good start."

She looked around at the chickens and back to him. "So, you're saying we're connected then?"

He got that serious look in his eyes again, the one that made her shiver and wonder if maybe those strange thoughts weren't completely ludicrous. "I think we've been connected for a little while, haven't we?"

Frenchie thought back to that first night they had met, when he had chased her like some sort of serial killer. Then how he'd found her again in the park and chased her again.

She had been so sure that was the end of her life and the start of something truly horrendous, but it had been the opposite. She'd gotten a gym membership for protection, basically a vacation for two weeks, help for her friend, and several delicious meals. All in all, he was the best thing that had happened to her in years.

Which was a lot to think about as well.

"I guess you're right."

"I've been known to be occasionally."

"Did you ever think that some homeless vagrant defacing your family's property would ever become kinda your friend?"

"*Kinda*?" he repeated incredulously. "There's no kinda about it. You're my friend and that's that."

"Oh."

"Oh? Your tone implies you didn't know."

"Well, I just... I don't know. I guess, once I decided to trust you, I assumed I was more of a charity case than anything else. You know, someone helping you right a wrong, but not... not something so intimate as a friend."

He turned to her fully and his expression was even more intense. Whew! What gave him the right to look at her like that? It made her knees wobble a bit, which was so unlike her and a bit unsettling to say the least.

"You've been doing that this past couple of days. Why?" he asked.

"What do you mean?"

"This weird, putting yourself down thing. You've always been so fearlessly you, so what's going on?"

She flushed at the praise, because it certainly felt like praise. "I don't know. I guess sometimes I get self-conscious because you've turned into this great guy who's nice and examines his biases and is willing to go to bat for a bunch of us hooligans, and I'm just... well, I'm a twenty-three-year-old woman with a sixteen-year-old's education. I'm trying to put the pieces together, but I really should have been out of this cycle by now, and I don't really have any excuses for why I'm not. It just seems like every time I get close to getting back on my feet, something knocks me down again."

She risked a look at him even though her cheeks were burning, and she felt nauseous. Showing vulnerability was so unlike her. She preferred her constant wit and sarcasm, fortifiers of the enormous wall that she had built around herself. But Solomon deserved the truth, or at least a little bit of it.

"Sometimes, it's hard to look at someone as successful as you and not feel like a loser."

"Frenchie…"

She hadn't known what to expect from her comment, but it wasn't for him to stride forward and envelop her in another hug.

It was a bit different than the first hug. For one, he held her tighter; secondly, she felt his lips press into the top of her head.

Oh.

Oh.

She knew it was most likely meant to be a sweet gesture, something paternal even, but it made her whole-body rush and her toes curl inside of her ratty shoes. It was something she hadn't felt since she was in high school, and boy, it certainly was powerful.

She had it even worse than she thought.

Yikes.

She pulled away slowly, looking up at his face, and she wished that she could be anybody else. But she wasn't. She was her, and that was all she had.

"Do you want to know my real name?"

19

———————

Solomon

Frenchie looked up at him, so beautiful, so wounded, and then her full lips were moving, and low, raspy words were escaping her mouth.

"Do you want to know my real name?"

Her real name? He hadn't realized that he didn't, she was just so much *Frenchie* in his head. It summed up her wry wit, her mischievousness, and so much more. But then again, hadn't she been surprised that he had told her his real name when they had first met? Yeah, he distinctly remembered her saying something along those lines.

"I want to know anything about you that you're willing to share with me."

She was so small in his hands. Even after two weeks of eating regularly and resting, he could still see that she could stand to gain a bit more weight. He felt a desire to protect her that was so strong it nearly stole his breath away, and he was surprised he didn't say something stupid right then and there.

"It's nothing too surprising, just Francesca. Francesca Lopez."

"Francesca," he repeated. It was beautiful, just like her. He wished he could trace the slope of her face with his fingers, commit all of her to memory.

Because eventually she was going to disappear, right? He was just a visitor in her world, a temporary ally while he helped her punish the man who had hurt her and her friends. He wasn't a permanent fixture, and he needed to come to terms with that before he hurt himself.

Except he kind of had a feeling he was going to hurt no matter what when she slipped away.

"I like it," he murmured, his hands coming up to stroke her arms. He wasn't really thinking about what he was doing. He wanted to hug her again, to comfort her and make whatever was influencing her to doubt herself go away. Sure, it was nice to hear that she thought such nice things about him, but none of them were really true.

Okay, yeah, from an outside view he was successful, but he had been born with so many advantages. If he had to deal with any of the issues the young ones had to deal with, he didn't know if that would be the case. Because, as much as he liked to think that he was ambitious, intelligent, and capable, he'd never really been tested in his entire life. He'd never known what it was like to be hungry with no hope of a meal. He'd always had two parents, a nice roof over his head and no worries about where his clothes or food would come from.

If he had been an immigrant, or poor, or abused, he likely wouldn't be in the same position he was in. So what kind of success was that? No, something that he actually felt proud of was helping Frenchie lock that man away, and he would feel even prouder if they managed to keep him there.

"Well, at least one of us likes my name. Always felt too fancy to me," Frenchie said.

"Does it?"

She nodded, her breath brushing against his face. It would be so easy to kiss her, to press her against him and feel her heartbeat through her ribs. The image of her without her shirt flared into his mind. and he scolded himself. The memory of what had caused that particular misunderstanding made him take a step back.

He wasn't going to be like all those people who had tried to use her. He wasn't going to be like the man from the food pantry who preyed on those who were weaker than him. Yes, he was drawn to the woman in a way that he couldn't describe, but that didn't mean he had the right to paw at her. And what if she thought she couldn't refuse him without endangering her relationship with the lawyers and everything else?

Ugh, the thought gave him chills. No, she was off-limits, and that was the long and the short of it.

"Well, shall we go inside? I can make us some coffee before we wake up the others and head back to the city."

"Coffee?" she said, her face breaking into a wide smile. "Now you're speaking my language. Let's go."

"All right then." Although he knew better, he still offered her his arm. She took it, wrapping her much smaller one around his. He could see the beginning of a bicep forming on her arm, and it looked so natural there. Healthy, like she finally had the fuel for her body to do what it wanted. "Let's head inside."

It was almost like she curled into his side as they walked along, her warm form reminding him of the things he was trying not to think about. Once they were inside, he went about fixing her a cup of coffee, pleased to see that the house staff had already cleaned everything up and packed the leftovers up for Frenchie. He needed to look into their pay again, make sure that they were being compensated appropriately. He had always assumed that they were, considering his family paid above minimum wage, but he was quickly learning that often that just wasn't enough.

Frenchie, because she would always be Frenchie to him, hopped up on a stool and quickly changed the subject onto something about horses. He was only catching about two-thirds of what she was saying, his mind too distracted by everything that had happened.

She noticed, of course, because nothing got by Frenchie, but she didn't say anything. Instead, she just kept up the conversation for both of them while he sipped his coffee and observed her. She really was a force of nature. What would have become of his life if he had never stepped into her path?

He didn't know, and he couldn't help but feel like God had put him there for a reason. But he couldn't figure out what that reason could be if they were going to eventually move apart to their separate worlds again. That seemed far too cruel.

"Do I have something in my teeth?" she asked.

"Huh, no. Just thinking."

"I could tell by all the steam coming out of your ears. You okay over there?"

He laughed and poured himself another cup of the dark roast. It was a special kind, one that Sal ordered from Europe because of the unique flavor. "You want more?"

"Um, yes. Not to be a broken record, but rich-people coffee is great."

He chuckled at that. He thought he would be a bit annoyed

or sheepish that they kept pointing out every single thing as being insane, especially the little things that he never thought of, but it was making him take better inventory of everything around him. Made him more grateful, appreciative. But it also made him kind of sad. He didn't like that these kids were amazed at soft sheets or multiple beds. It just didn't seem right for his family to have so much while they didn't even have family.

"Let's go wake up the others. It's been about an hour and a half. That should be enough for a good lie down," Solomon said.

"I don't know about you, but given that they're all on really comfy beds, they could probably sleep for a few hours."

"Oh, should we let them then? You and I could watch a movie," he said.

Then again, that might not be the best idea. Sitting alone with her in their dark home theater, reclined in their comfortable chairs, right next to each other... that probably was a temptation he would do better without.

Frenchie shook her head. "Hmm, I'm afraid if I do that, that I won't want to get up again. And, no offense, but I don't really want to run into your father. I assume you brought us all over here this afternoon because he's out."

"Yeah, at a golfing tournament. Probably won't be back until late."

"Really? Isn't it difficult to golf in the dark?"

"Oh, they finish at a good time but usually end up drinking around the bar for hours and schmoozing. You know, comparing stories about the good old days."

Frenchie nodded. "They mean the days that were good to them. I mean, I'm willing to bet that things are still pretty good for them."

"You're not wrong."

"I'm usually not," she gave him a wink then started to flounce upstairs. It was borderline indescribably nice to see her relax around him, begin to trust him. He never would have thought he would be on the list of people she allowed to see the real version of herself.

It was a pretty big honor, and he wasn't going to take that for granted.

WAKING THEM UP, driving the lot home, and coming back ended up taking about three hours in total. But that might have been because he insisted on stopping at a fast food place and loading then up with more food. True, they still had the leftovers from lunch, but he figured some of them were teenagers and, therefore, bottomless pits.

He was right too, because they sucked the junk food down within seconds. It made him want to get more vegetables in them, but he understood that those weren't as filling as straight-up carbs and protein.

And it also didn't help that he and Frenchie lingered at the door, talking, joking. He didn't want to say goodbye, and eventually it was her that ended up having to end the conversation, saying she needed to get more applications in while she still had access to the internet and the hotel phone.

"You know, it's going to be really hard to keep tracking all of you down after this week ends, and the lawyers said they still want to meet with you a couple more times. You should stay here until that's all settled."

A strange look crossed her face. "Solomon… you can't keep paying for this place forever."

"Actually, I definitely can." She didn't smile at his joke. "Look, I just really want this guy to pay for what he's done. Being able to connect with you easily will be a huge help."

"I... all right. But I can't keep staying in this bubble forever. It's going to spoil me."

Maybe she deserved to be a little spoiled.

But he'd kept that thought to himself and headed back home, more tired than he thought he would be and with his head full of thoughts.

"Hey there, stranger. Haven't seen you around as much lately."

Solomon looked around, recognizing the voice of his brother but not seeing him. A sharp rap caught his attention, and he glanced out of the window of the garage to see Silas on his horse.

"Hey," he answered, sliding the glass up. "You hit the stables?"

"Yeah, I caught sight of you doing it last week, and I was reminded that it's been a right long time since I visited my old girl." He patted his horse's neck, an unusually large mare with the prettiest black and grey dappling.

"Where's Sterling? He go to the stables too?"

"Nah, Father hauled him to the tournament. I went the last time, so it's his turn. Besides, it's not like most of those people can tell us apart. They're so busy trying to get into our pockets that it really doesn't matter which one we are."

"That's a mood," Solomon said before cracking a smile. He was picking up on some of the teenager's lingo. He didn't know if that was a good thing or not, but it still made a strange sort of warmth spread through his chest.

"But hey, my twin's suffering aside, I've been meaning to ask you, is something going on?"

"What do you mean?"

"Well, I know you pretty much run things around here, but I'm a part of the structure too." That was true. While none of his brothers worked full time for the McLintoc Miller LLC, Silas liked to spend his time in acquisitions and real estate. He had a real knack for spotting good properties and had been the one to originally hear about the megachurch needing repairs after the last tornado and had gotten that ball rolling. "And I couldn't help but notice that you yoinked a couple of my favorite lawyers and even hired on some criminal justice folks from the city. Kinda weird, you know?"

Solomon didn't like lying, and as easy as it would be to make up some reason to his next-youngest brother, Silas deserved the truth.

"The food pantry connected to that church was being used by a predator to target young women who went there. Dad wanted to make the victims go away with hush money and shuffle the man off where he could do less harm."

Just like Solomon, Silas was quiet for a moment, his eyes flashing wide before returning to neutral. He always did have a great poker face. "And you're absolutely certain this happened?"

"I got an attempted assault on camera and recorded. I saw the injuries of another girl he attacked. The guy is an animal."

"Ah, so I take it you're not gonna do what Dad asked?"

"No. I'm doing the opposite."

"He's not gonna like that."

"I'm aware."

Silas cracked a small grin. "First Samuel, then you. It's interesting all these changes are happening. Makes ya wonder, doesn't it?"

"What is it supposed to make me wonder, exactly?"

"If we're going about this all wrong. I mean, our cousins aren't as well off as us, but they're a heck of a lot happier, I would say. And they've all found true love, it seems. Meanwhile, we're all single despite being what most people would call attractive."

"Are you saying you're a romantic, Silas?" Solomon asked, deflecting from himself. Because his younger brother's words hit home.

Uncle and Aunt Miller's branch of the family did seem to be happier, even with some of the tough stuff they were handed. Like their second oldest having some really serious PTSD and their youngest being exiled from the family but then coming back. He wasn't quite sure on that, but they seemed mostly hunky-dory now.

"Nah, never much saw the point in it. But I'm thinking maybe you do."

"I... you calling me out, Silas?"

"Nah, you know how I am. I always like to ask 'what if.' Anyways, I'm going to enjoy the rest of my ride with my girl. It sounds like you might have a lot to think about."

Solomon shook his head and closed the window as his brother rode off onto one of the paths at the back of the house. Old trails that they used to ride all the time but that were barely used lately.

Figures one of the twins would fill his head with even more stuff to puzzle over. They'd always been some oddballs.

Oddballs who had a habit of being annoyingly right.

But the blatant truth was that he had feelings for Frenchie, feelings that he couldn't act on while he was in a position of power over her. And holding the means to her hotel suite, her place of living, was definitely a position of power. Not to mention being in charge of the lawyers representing her case.

So he could only be her friend—not that that was a bad thing—until everything was taken care of. In the meantime, he would continue to help her flourish and learn more about what the 'real world' was like.

And who knew, maybe life would do the impossible. Maybe he could help Frenchie turn things around. Then maybe, just maybe, she'd end up letting him into her life for good.

20

Frenchie

Frenchie had forgotten what it was like to go to bed every night cold and hungry with an ache so deep in her bones that it might never come out.

She had forgotten what it was like to wake up on the ground with only her blanket and hoody, wishing for something soft to rest against.

She had forgotten just how exhausting it was to constantly be searching for resources, and the boredom that came with being too hungry and tired to entertain herself.

She had forgotten everything that she'd spent years numbing herself to, but now she was looking all of that in the face again.

It was the week before Thanksgiving and somehow, the lawyers had managed to strike a deal with the animal that hurt Tawny. It was incredible timing, only about a month and a half after he was arrested, and Frenchie had been under the impression that it would take much, much longer.

So it was a relief to be out from under the bad guy's shadow, but much less of a relief because they didn't need the suite anymore. There was no need for Solomon to keep looking out for them.

That left a bittersweet taste in her mouth. Frenchie liked being independent, she liked not relying on anybody but herself, but she also didn't want her path to diverge from his. They were like two comets shooting in opposite directions who only managed to line up for a little while.

But even if it had only been a short few months, she cherished them dearly. Also, not to forget that he'd given her the resources to take several big steps she'd been struggling with.

She'd gone to three interviews and gotten a part-time job at a big box store. It wasn't the most amazing pay, but it was a dollar above minimum wage, and she got at least twenty hours a week. When Solomon had heard, he'd taken her shopping to buy plenty of new outfits for the job. She'd fought him a bit on it before realizing that he liked giving her things and she shouldn't spoil his fun. Spending money on frivolous things was still so stressful to her.

She still had her gym membership, so she wasn't worried about freezing to death in the night. She had a job, *and* she'd managed to get herself a library card! The new library was truly massive, and they even had 3D printers there, which was absolutely wild. Strangely enough, one of the librarians recognized her so they got to talking, and the next thing Frenchie knew, she was signing up for a GED program.

So yeah, things were looking on the up and up.

...except for that whole being homeless thing again.

What if she had gotten soft? She had gained almost

enough weight to feel like her real self again, but she still wanted to add on much more muscle. She'd even managed to get to the local cosmetology school and get her hair touched up. The person had wanted to practice their ombre technique, so currently she had red to orange to yellow hair like fire. She loved it, and it made her feel a bit more like herself.

"I'm gonna miss this place," Tawny said, running her thumb across her teeth. It was a habit she'd started up ever since Solomon took her to get her teeth fixed that had been chipped in the attack. Frenchie didn't even want to *think* about how much that must have cost, considering the repairs were pretty much seamless. "If you woulda told me I went from being beaten nearly to death to living in the lap of luxury, I woulda told you that you were insane."

"This isn't the lap of luxury, Tawny."

"Oh, you're right. That would be Solomon's guest rooms. Those beds are *commmfy*."

Tawny wasn't wrong. The meetings with the lawyers had both run long, and Solomon had his staff feed them both times, resulting in naps by everyone the second time around. Frenchie had tried to resist, but Tawny had pulled her down onto one of the beds and then it was lights out.

"Do you think he's going to rush in at the last minute and whisk you off like some sort of Prince Charming?"

"Prince Charmings aren't real, Tawny, and hoping for things just ends up hurting you in the long run."

"Geez, someone woke up on the wrong side of the bed. You okay?"

"I'm fine," she groused. "Let's just—"

A knock sounded at the door, nearly startling her out of her pants. Tawny mouthed a question asking who it could be, but Frenchie had no idea. Carefully, she went to the door and looked out the peephole. Surprisingly enough, it was Solomon.

Strange. When he hadn't talked to them about renewing their time at the suite yet again, she assumed he was finally done being their host. Which was fine. He'd spent a ridiculous amount of money on them already. She had known that it was coming, and yet it still stung so hard.

"Uh, hey there," she said uncertainly as she opened the door. "Wasn't expecting you."

"You think I'm gonna let you guys fend for yourself on move-out day? That would be rude." Maybe, but it was incredibly awkward that he was there. "So, where are you guys off to?" He walked in, grabbing both her backpack and the one that Tawny had scrounged up. With her first paycheck, Frenchie had bought them both small coolers, some nicer jackets from the thrift shop, and duffle bags they could sling over their shoulders to carry along with their backpacks.

They'd need to find ways to hide both the coolers and duffles, because walking around with them definitely made them a target, but Frenchie was pretty good at burying things and remembering where they were left. She'd only lost one cache, and it was because a building was being built over it while she had been on the road with a carnival.

And the containers were worth the extra struggle just so they didn't have to leave everything behind. With everything that Solomon had been buying for them, or her new situation had allowed her to buy for herself, she had far too much to live out of only a backpack. It was nice, having multiple outfits and all of her toiletries in full portions rather than sample sizes she nicked a few extra of when they were being given out at the shelter.

"All right, I'll take these to the truck then come back up for the rest."

He hurried off, leaving Frenchie and Tawny standing there, looking after him.

"This is weird, right?" Tawny asked in a slow drawl. "Because this feels weird."

"It's definitely weird."

"Glad it's not just me then."

They didn't continue any further than that, because then Solomon was coming back up to grab the rest. Frenchie lingered as she went to close the door for the last time. She found herself getting emotional, tears prickling at the corner of her eyes. The suite had come to mean a lot to her. It was where her life had changed, pretty much. Where she had found out that maybe, just maybe, she could be worth more to someone than her pound of flesh.

But that was the trouble with things mattering; they hurt when they eventually got taken away.

Pushing the melancholy down and forcing herself to be grateful she'd ever had the suite at all, Frenchie closed the door, the key card inside on the table for the housekeeper to clean up.

And that was it. An insane chapter of her life was closed, and she was onto new and important things.

If she kept working hard, she could probably afford a studio in a month or so. Security deposits were always the worst, and she knew with her lack of credit that she was going to have to pay first and last month's rent as well. She was doing well at her job, and although it was too early to tell, she was pretty sure they'd keep her on for at least a few hours a week after the holidays.

"So, where am I taking you to?" Solomon asked, strangely

cheerful as they all got into another one of his work vans. There was hardly enough room for her in the front and Tawny in the back, the van jack packed with various furniture items and bags. Clearly it had been in the middle of a job when he had borrowed the vehicle. He could have waited for whoever they were to finish.

"Tawny is going over to the factory area past the public market. I'm heading to the park."

"Oh, the two of you didn't manage to land shelter spots?"

"No, they're usually at a premium during the winter, and the ones that aren't are first come, first serve every night."

"Huh. All right."

...that was strange. Normally Solomon got all uncomfortable like whenever they were talking about her being on the streets, but he was acting like everything was normal. Was he just trying to be chill and massively overcompensating? If so, he needed to knock it off.

She looked out the window, deep in thought. She was so wrapped up in her complex feelings that she didn't realize that something was amiss for a good handful of minutes.

"Uh, Solomon? Where are you going? This isn't the way to the park or the factory area."

"Oh, it isn't? I must have taken a wrong turn. Hold on."

Except he didn't try to turn after that and seemed to know exactly where he was going.

Frenchie wasn't stupid. She could tell that something was up but had no idea what. He hadn't... planned a surprise party or something bizarre, right? Because on top of everything else, that would be far too much.

Strangely enough, she still didn't get an answer as he pulled to the side on a random block in a neighborhood. It wasn't high-class or even middle-class, but it wasn't rundown either. The sidewalks were mostly intact, and she saw signs that the people around took pride in their houses, and the buildings weren't dilapidated or falling apart.

"What are we doing?" she asked, trying to keep her tone normal. In reality, she was a bit irritated. She wanted to get this whole saying goodbye thing over with so she could breathe again. Because, at the moment, it felt like her heart was squeezing painfully in her chest.

"Oh, I hope you don't mind, but I needed to stop in and sign some forms for one of our workers. You should come with. I heard his cat had kittens."

She wanted to say no, that she could wait, but a squeal sounded from the back. "Oh, *kittens! WHERE?*" And then Tawny was vaulting out of the side door like a track star.

Of course, Frenchie wasn't going to sit alone in the van like some sort of spoilsport, so she followed after. But they only went a few steps before Solomon slowed to a stop, just facing a house.

"What?" she asked, looking it over. It was a nice place, that was for certain. Two floors with what looked like one of those older attics on top. Storm porch. Looked like there was plenty of room for whatever employee Solomon was visiting and his family. There was even a yard in the back.

"So, what do you think?"

"Huh? Uh, it's nice."

"Good, that makes things easier." Before she could ask him what he meant, he kept on talking. "Because it's yours."

...what?

She stared at him, sure that she was having a stroke, but now he really seemed to be pulling out a roll of paper from under his arm. Since when had that even been there?

"This is the paperwork for this house to be entirely in your own name. I also have some track phones with minutes cards in the car. I took care of the utilities for the first few months, and you're taken care of on taxes for this year."

"I... I don't understand."

"I want you to be able to take care of yourself, and I understand that—while I liked providing for you through this stressful time lately—you're an independent sort of person who likes to take care of herself. Also, this way, you are in control of your own housing, your own life, and what you do with them."

"Oh, and Tawny, I managed to get you a part-time job at the local learning center with the caveat that you attend some lessons there. Mostly just cleaning and organization, but it'll give you pocket money and help you catch up with the studies you've missed."

The girl was staring at him with the same shocked expression that Frenchie was wearing, so she knew she wasn't hallucinating everything the man was saying.

"But won't they have to report me?"

"Texas has some different laws regarding emancipation than New York. And while your parents live in good old NY, by the time they got down here and contested it, you'd be eighteen and everything would be a moot point."

"Oh. Wow. Huh. You've really thought of everything, haven't you?"

"I just want the two of you to get back on your feet and do all the things that I know you can do. This way, at least you have a fairer start."

Frenchie didn't know what to do, didn't know what to say, she didn't even know what to think. So instead she just threw herself at him in a hug, crushing his form to hers with all the strength in her body.

She was so overwhelmed with the feeling of it all, the gratitude, and the relief that he wasn't trying to get rid of her. No, he was just sneakily planning on completely turning her life around even more than she thought was possible.

What had she ever done to deserve such kindness? She wasn't smart, or particularly talented, and yet someone like *him* was seemingly willing to move heaven and earth to set her up well.

She wasn't thinking when her hands went to either side of his head, wanting to pull him down into a kiss, wanting him to feel how happy he made her. And not just because he got her nice things—*incredible things*—but because he cared enough to do so.

Her heart was so full, but that feeling cracked when he stiffened and pulled away, his large hands coming up to pull hers away from his face.

"What... what's wrong?" she asked. Had she been imagining those intense looks? Was she completely wrong about everything? Did he only see her as a charity case and nothing else?

He shook his head, looking like he was struggling with the right words himself. "It's just... I... I did this because I care for you. And I don't want you to feel like you owe me, okay. I'm still not like those people."

Oh. He was remembering the first time in the suite together, where she had thought that he would only help Tawny if she gave herself to him. That moment still caused embarrassment to rush through her, but how else was she supposed to know back then that he was basically a Christmas miracle in human flesh?

"I know. And I know you never could be. I know it took me a while, but I don't think that way anymore."

The look of surprise, of absolute relief that washed over him was visible from even where she was standing. "Is that really true?"

"I wouldn't say it if it wasn't."

"Well... in that case, if you were open to it, I... I'd like to court you. Like you're supposed to court a lady."

Oh, a lady now, was she? That was something she hadn't been called before. "And what exactly does courting a lady entail?"

He blushed and goodness, that was a great look across his cheeks. "Well, mostly it starts with a date, no more contact than maybe holding hands. Good conversation. Good food. Maybe some fancy lighting. Flowers."

She smiled from ear to ear, almost worried that her face might crack. "That sounds lovely to me," she murmured, her heart swelling in her chest. But then, out of nowhere, a cry of frustration sounded from behind her.

"Aw, *man!*" Tawny said.

Frenchie whirled around, raising her eyebrows. "What?"

Tawny was squinting angrily. "There never were any kittens, were there?"

21

———

Solomon

It was a strange thing to realize that, at thirty-three years old, he'd never been on a date that he wanted to be on just because he liked a person. Sure, he had dated around more when he was younger, and then again in college, but it had almost always been for a goal. Either to try out new restaurants or political mergers or currying favor. He'd always been so obsessed with the business side of things that he'd forgotten that dating could just be for fun.

Or because he had intense feelings for a woman that he maybe shouldn't have.

Except that factor was gone now, wasn't it? He no longer controlled her housing, or anything of hers really. Sure, he had gotten that freedom by just buying a bunch of things for her, but the important thing was that he couldn't take them back.

She was entirely the legal owner of her house, her phone, and she had gone and gotten herself a job on her own.

And in fact, it was *her* house that he was driving to, to pick her up to take her to their nice meal at a steakhouse in town.

It wasn't the high-end one that his family would normally visit, but he figured that would be too much for Frenchie on their first date. The first of hopefully many others if he had any wishes left.

So they were going to a mid-tier one, one where he could still feel like he was treating her but not so extreme that she might feel like he was bragging. It was a delicate balance that he wasn't that familiar with.

But she was worth it. More than anyone else he knew.

When he arrived at her house, he found her waiting at the doorway of her porch. *Her* porch, an idea that made him feel happy and content inside. No matter what happened with them, she had a home. A place to call her own.

"Hey there," he said, handing her the flowers he got. They were a simple collection of summer flowers, no doubt things she missed with it being the colder months. "You look lovely."

"Thanks. You bought the clothes."

"That's not what I mean, and I'm pretty sure you know that."

"Yeah, I do." She took the flowers and buried her face in them.

That made his chest swell with some sort of weird, caveman pride.

She smiled. "I'll go put these in a vase. Because of course you bought us a vase."

He smiled crookedly. "I tried to get you everything you could need."

"Well, you've done a good job so far. I'm still unpacking and finding things."

"Yeah... I might have gone a little overboard. Potentially." He hadn't. He had bought her only half of what he originally wanted, and that was being conservative. He had a long, long wish list of items saved online for—actually, he wasn't sure what. Maybe Christmas? A rainy day? He wasn't sure, but if their date went well, hopefully he would have more chances to give her little presents.

...or big presents. Like a fully lit vanity or a huge dresser with extra room for all the clothes she might buy as time went along.

"You okay? Earth to Solomon. I put the flowers in the vase. Ready to go?"

He blinked. He hadn't realized that he had been lost in his thoughts, but he quickly flashed her a grin.

"That I am. Let's go."

She returned his grin, albeit nervously, and they headed outside. She let him open her door for her, and when he slid into the truck, she was giggling.

"What?" he asked.

"Nothing. I just... I've never been on a date. I've always told myself I didn't care because it was cheesy, but I dunno... it's kinda nice."

"Glad you think so."

He started the truck and pulled away, going the speed limit for once. He wasn't in a hurry, wanting to make the most of every moment with Frenchie. Apparently, as the holidays ramped up, so did her hours at her job. Sometimes he was tempted to tell her to just call in so she could actually enjoy her new place, but that was exactly what he had been trying to avoid.

"So, how have things been on the ranch? Decidedly more ranchy?"

He laughed at the word. "Yeah, actually. Even though it's winter and that's usually when things slow down. Just wait until spring comes around, Mom would love to show you her garden."

"Oh, so you want to introduce me to your parents then?"

He gave her a wide-eyed look. "Wait, you'd want to meet my—Oh. You're kidding. You're teasing me right now."

She laughed, throwing her head back and letting out long peals of mirth. "Yes, I am. Sorry, am I being terrible?"

"The absolute worst."

"Well, guess you better turn around and take me back," she said with a cheeky grin.

"All right, maybe not the *worst*. But there's always room for improvement."

"Isn't that the truth?" she said, tone suddenly serious. "But I feel like ever since I met you, that's all I've been doing."

Wow... that was a compliment and a half, and he tried not to preen too much at it. He didn't even know if Frenchie was aware of just how important those words were.

He loved the way she made him feel. More connected and normal. There weren't goals and discussions. No mergers or political winds. Just two people enjoying each other's company for the sake of enjoyment.

They continued to talk as they drove along, just casual things about her work and how Tawny was doing with the first week of her program. The young girl was excited to be back, even if she was still nervous about her parents finding her.

But he had a good feeling that they wouldn't do anything. It was too close to her eighteenth birthday, and the learning center made it clear that they legally could consider her emancipated and not report her.

They arrived in good time, and he actually parked his car. He was so used to using valet services that it was a bit of a novel experience for him, but he knew better than to say so. There was only so much good-natured ribbing he could get before he started to feel stupid or out of touch.

Even though he *was* out of touch. But he was learning. Bit by bit, he was learning.

For example, it had been exceedingly difficult to get Frenchie to buy one of the nice, insulated coats he recommended to her. They weren't a bad price, around a hundred and twenty each because they were on clearance, but they were warm, durable and even waterproof. It would last her for a decade or two as opposed to the fifteen dollar one she wanted from the thrift store that would last maybe a year or two.

It had been a very long conversation where she explained, since she was buying something for Tawny and herself, that she would never have the disposable income to spend over two hundred dollars on coats, even if they lasted forever. The most she could afford was what was at the thrift store, and even if those turned out to be more in the long run, that was just how it was.

He'd offered to buy the coats for her, of course, but she'd been strangely adamant that she had to do it herself. That was right around when he got the feeling that, as much as he liked getting her things, she was used to taking care of herself and he was reaching the end of her coddling-limit.

So he'd backed off and learned more about how the poor stayed poor. It wasn't bad buying choices; it was that they literally couldn't afford the good choices because they just didn't have enough capital. It made so much more sense than his father insisting that they all were just after instant gratification.

"Wow, this place smells delicious," she murmured from the parking lot. Even in the low light, he could see how wide her pupils were in anticipation of a good meal.

"Wait until you're inside."

She nodded, taking his arm again as they headed toward the door.

He was right. The restaurant was a great choice. For one, they didn't have their prices on the menu, and secondly, they had a broad range of options. Frenchie ended up getting the surf and turf at his recommendation while he decided on their slow-cooked brisket. It had nothing on his Aunt Annie's recipe, but it was still quite delicious, and they spent the entire meal laughing and joking with each other.

There was no talk of predators or legal things, no talk of rich or poor. Just the two of them, as equals, being in the moment and enjoying a good meal together.

It was worth absolutely every cent, and they ended up staying almost until close even though Frenchie had said she had work in the morning. It made him feel a touch guilty about that, but she seemed to be enjoying herself just as much as he was.

As he took her home, he found himself wanting the moment to last longer. To whisk her off into a world where she didn't have to worry about money or bills or anything like that. But he also respected her need to have her own goals and accomplishments.

So he maybe took one or two wrong turns on the way back to her house. But only that, because he really did want her to get a good night's rest.

He pulled up to her house and didn't miss how her face still lit up when she looked at it. He supposed she was still getting used to it, to having something so important to her name. Good, he was glad that he was able to make her happy, no matter what happened between them.

"I suppose this is goodnight," he said.

"Yeah, I suppose it is."

He went around the truck and opened her door, offering his hand to help her out. They walked together to her front door where they stopped again, her head turned up to look at him.

"Thank you for tonight. For everything. I had a lot of fun," she said.

"Enough fun to want to do this again?"

She flushed and wow, if she was beautiful normally, she was even more so when she was well-fed and blushing. "Yeah. I could see myself wanting a repeat of tonight."

"All right, but only if you cook for me again. I loved that spicy cabbage you made."

"Spicy... it was seasoned with salt and pepper! How is that spicy?!"

"I have a delicate palate," he retorted. That wasn't true at all. He quite liked spicy things; he just hadn't expected cabbage to actually taste good.

"Sure, you do." They shared another laugh that eventually petered out, leaving them staring at each other, the tension between them rising again. "So... does this courting thing allow for goodnight kisses?"

That hadn't been what he was expecting, and his blood rushed within his veins. "I... I think that might be all right."

"Good. Because I'd really like that."

His hands came up, cupping her face, tilting it up towards him. He hesitated a moment, looking at her every feature, drinking it all in because he didn't want to forget a single detail. And then, he lowered his head so that their lips were pressed against each others.

Even as much as he had thought about touching her, thought about the feel of her against him, he still wasn't prepared. His entire body filled with heat while her lips were soft and petallike against his.

She let out a sound, a soft, vulnerable little sound that made his body pump with adrenaline. His hands dropped from her face to wind around her, pressing her into him, feeling her body flush with his.

Then he had to pull himself away.

"You didn't have to stop," Frenchie murmured, her eyes half-lidded. And wow, as if that wasn't a *look* for her. Her lips were red and puffy looking, her cheeks were flushed, and her breath was coming in a sort of raspy rush.

"Nah, I was serious about wanting to do this the right way."

"Why are you so set on this courting thing? It's not like I'm some virgin, or a fancy, do-good lady. Sure, you set me up with some things, but I'm just a homeless girl from the system."

His hands found her face again, and he leaned down so he could rest his forehead against hers.

"You are so much more than that and you're worth treating right." He pulled his head away and placed a kiss where his forehead had just been resting. "You're worth taking the time for. You're worth treating as a precious, important person." Another little kiss and she sighed, sagging against him. "I promise you, I'm going to prove that I can be worthy of a woman who's as incredible, as strong as you."

"I..." Her breath hitched, and he thought he might feel something damp against his shirt. "Okay. If you want to try, I'm game. But for the record, that's a pretty intense thing to prove."

"Don't worry. I'm up for it."

EPILOGUE

Frenchie

Frenchie bounced her leg as she sat in a pew, a single piece of paper in her hand. She was in the church that was just a block away from her library, not many people there since it was Wednesday.

"Can I help you, miss?"

She looked up to see a kind woman standing at the end of the pew. It wasn't the sort of question she was used to, as most churches in the area were pretty against homeless people lurking around after hours for shelter.

"Uh, no. Just have a lot to think about."

"That so?" She slid into the pew and sat a respectable distance away. "Anything you want to talk about?"

"I'm sure you wouldn't understand."

"Well, why don't you try me?"

Frenchie took a long, deep breath. "Well, it's just that I've lived the past five years as sort of a non-existing person. I was so focused on survival that I didn't have time for much else. But now..."

"Now what?"

"Well now... there's *everything*. I've got a house. I've been hired on fulltime at my job. I've been dating this amazing guy for six months now, and I've had the most perfect Christmas I could ever ask for."

It really had been beautiful. She'd cried a couple of times. And meeting his family had only been mildly terrifying, if by mildly she meant completely and totally to the point where she'd gotten nauseous almost instantly. But it was better than anything that she could ask for.

"And that has given you something to think about?"

"Yeah, because you see, I kind of just got my official GED certificate today, and I'm only just now realizing that I might actually be a woman of worth."

"And that wasn't something you considered yourself before?"

"Well... no. I was just a street kid turned street woman. But now I have all these things, and all these paths are open to me. I kind of... just don't know what to do. I don't want to waste it."

"Ah, I see. That's a pretty big series of changes."

"It is." It was terrifying. It was wonderful. It was everything she had ever wanted, but it had been out of her reach for so long that she didn't know what to do now that she had accomplished her goals.

"Well, I would think that, for the moment, do you have to do anything at all?"

Frenchie looked at her suspiciously. "What do you mean?"

"Well, you've been working this whole time, struggling

every day. And now that you've accomplished everything that you're supposed to do, maybe you deserve a break."

"But... I didn't get there on my own. I was helped a lot. I mean, there was a reason that even after five years I couldn't end up anywhere."

"That doesn't matter. When a doctor saves a life, do we discredit them because their teachers gave them the knowledge to succeed? Do we discredit him because he needed the help of the nurses and all the support staff in order to do anything?

"No. We don't. Because some things require a team. No matter who helped you out, you deserve time to celebrate everything you've accomplished."

Frenchie nodded her head, thinking about what the woman said.

The woman continued, "Or... if you're feeling particularly ambitious, maybe you can use this time to take a risk that you wouldn't normally."

"Come again?"

"I've never been homeless, but I've been in some tough situations. And I know that afterward is usually when all that adrenaline and relief help your mind figure out what you really want to do. Something that you could never do or have when you were so busy fighting just to survive the day. I'm sure there's something in that head of yours that you might like to do, but never had the resources or strength to do before."

Frenchie chewed at her lips, looking down at the GED in her hands. It was proof that she wasn't an idiot. She'd finished the last year of high school education in an incredibly short time, and only because she tested so high when she entered the program. Apparently, she wasn't as stupid or as useless as she sometimes thought in the dead of night.

"Yeah… I can think of a few things." She heaved a sigh and stood, looking to the front of the church where a cross stood made of plain and simple wood. "You know, I never really cared about religion, or Jesus stuff. But I came here when I was confused. Solomon, you know, he seems to get a lot of comfort from the church, but I didn't expect it to work for me."

The woman just smiled, her face soft and kind. "It's interesting how that happens, isn't it?"

"Yeah. Thank you, ma'am."

Frenchie folded her paper and shoved it in her pocket. It wasn't actually the *real* certificate, just the confirmation that she had completed all of her tests and assignments and had a passing grade. She would laminate it at the library, but first she had something to do.

Pulling out her phone, she dialed up Solomon and he answered on the first ring. "Frenchie, what's up? Are you all right?"

"Oh yes. Fine. Just wondering where you are. At the Ranch?"

"No, actually. Dropping Simon off at the train station. He says he likes it better than flying because it doesn't make him as sick."

"So, you're in the city?"

"Yeah, about to leave though."

"Don't. Can you meet me somewhere? At that diner we first met up at?"

"Uh yeah, sure. If you need to."

"Yeah. I'll see you there."

She hung up and rushed off. She had the energy for it nowadays. After six months of finally being able to eat regularly, she was almost back to her athletic self. She had missed it. There was something about being in the body that she liked most that made her feel better every day. Could her biceps be bigger? Sure. But there was time for that later.

She made it to the diner, a sweaty, heaving mess, but it gave her time to get a table, a glass of water, and sit.

Solomon wasn't there too much later, sliding into the booth across from her with a smile on his face.

"So, what did you—" he started to ask.

"I love you."

Oh wow, she just went right out there and said it, didn't she? But since the dam was broken, everything else came pouring out. "I love you more than I've ever loved anyone else. You make me feel safe. You make me feel like I can do *anything*.

"And it's not just about how you make me feel. I want to talk to you, all the time. I want to find out about how your day is going. I want you to be happy and content. I want you to succeed and maybe fight with your father less often, and even though I don't see that happening, I support you."

"I..." He paused and seemed to take a deep breath, then smiled. "You chose a *diner* to do this?"

She barked out a surprised laugh. "Okay, maybe I didn't think about that. I dunno. It's a bit fitting though, isn't it?"

He nodded, his hands reaching forward to grip hers. "I love you too, Francesca Lopez. I've loved you since you first sat across this booth from me, I think."

"Oh..." She couldn't describe what that did for her. How that made her *feel*. "That's very good to hear."

"It is, isn't it?" he said with a grin. "So, do you want to get out of here, or are you hungry enough for a meal?"

"Well, I'd really like you to kiss me right now, but I'm never one to turn down a free meal."

"Fair enough. I think we can do both though."

He got up and slid in beside her, turning to her to place a

soft and tender kiss on her lips. As usual, it stole her breath away, and he was the one who had to break it off.

His arm went behind her head, supporting her and curling her to his strong side. She melted into him, knowing that she could trust him. Knowing that he would be there for her no matter what.

"You know, I've been struggling with something myself," he said, voice soft and low, floating through the little cloud they were in.

"Oh?" Frenchie asked, leaning her head against his shoulder. She felt so at peace that she couldn't help but be nervous that whatever he might say could pop the bubble, but she more than owed it to him to hear him out.

"Yeah. You know how when you try to do something perfectly, and you work it up into this big thing in your head and nothing is ever quite good enough?" Solomon said as Frenchie nodded. She knew that feeling all too well. "I guess I've been doing that myself."

"What with? Something with the business?"

He shook his head and then he was shifting, pulling something out of his back pocket. Before Frenchie could quite process it, he was sliding a small, blue box over to her.

"It's not an engagement ring," he said quickly. "I remember you saying you needed to date someone at least a year or two before you were ready for that."

"Then what is it?" her chest felt tight and her cheeks were flushing. Sure, he liked to shower her with gifts all the time, but something about the moment felt different.

"Open it."

Taking a deep breath, she did so, revealing a beautiful but understated ring of bright silver. There were no gems in it, but instead delicate engravings of vines and leaves. Definitely not an engagement ring, but not just any old ring either.

"I..."

"It's a promise ring." He held up his own hand, where a thicker and broader band already sat on one of his fingers. "You don't have to take it if you're not ready, but I wanted a physical sign that I believe in our future together. That if I'm going to end up with anyone in this world, it's going to be you, and only you."

Frenchie looked from him, and back to the ring. He was just so *good.* He listened. He understood her need to wait and be cautious. He also understood that there was always that fear in the back of her mind that he would grow tired of her. That she was temporary.

She was just so in *love.*

"Thank you!" she cried, throwing her arms around him and pulling him into a hug, not caring that the booth made it difficult. When they parted, he was sliding the ring on her finger and then they were kissing and maybe she was kinda crying again.

But it was wonderful. It wasn't a trap, it was a warm, comforting blanket that would always be with her. She was safe. She was loved. And knowing that they had a future together, no matter where it took them, was such an immense relief on her soul.

She finally felt like a real person now, and so was he, so the possibilities were endless.

And she couldn't wait to see what the future holds.

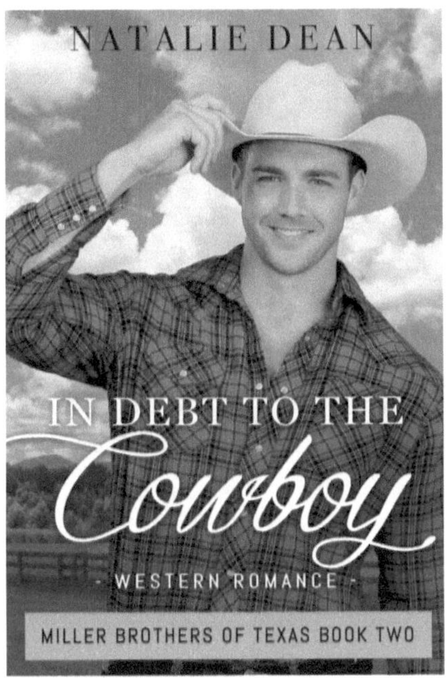

HELLO READER... I hope you enjoyed Solomon and Frenchie's love story. It sure was a different for me to do. As a matter of fact, out of all the stories I've written, this is the one I was the most unsure about. But I was happy to see readers still liked it! Thank you so much for still being here with me.

It's time for the next Miller story, In Debt to the Cowboy. I really love this one. Silas Miller meets his match when he meets Theodora, the spitfire mechanic who works on his vehicle.

You can find Silas and Theodora's love story on all major retailers. Plus, you can find it on my own online bookstore if you'd like to support my small mom-owned business. I'd be honored if you chose to do so. Scan the QR code below to be taken to In Debt to the Cowboy at Natalie Dean Books. If scanning QR codes isn't your thing, you can also find my store here: nataliedeanbooks.com

ABOUT THE AUTHOR

Born and raised in a small coastal town in the south, I was raised to treasure family and love the Lord. I'm a dedicated homeschooling mom who loves to travel and spend time with my growing-up-too-fast son.

When I'm not busy writing or running my business, you can find me cleaning house, cooking dinner, feeding our three rescue cats, trying to make learning fun and coaxing my son to pick up his toys. On less busy days, you may also find me paddling down a spring run in Florida, hiking a mountain trail in Georgia (on the rare vacation to the mountains), or enjoying a book.

If you love Natalie Dean books, you can be notified of new releases by signing up to my newsletter at nataliedeanau thor.com, where you will also receive two free short stories for signing up. Just click on the "Free Books" tab at the top and you'll be on your way!

Also, as previously mentioned, I've opened my own online bookstore and I'd love your support! As of June 2024, I'm selling my ebooks at Natalie Dean Books. By late summer or fall 2024, I should have audiobooks, regular paperbacks, large print paperbacks, dyslexic print paperbacks and signed paper- backs all available. At the request of my loyal readers, I'll also be adding merchandise, such as glasses, cups, magnets and more. So come check out my small mom-owned author busi- ness at nataliedeanbooks.com.

You can also scan the QR code below to be taken to the home page of Natalie Dean Books.

facebook.com/nataliedeanromance